EVIL NEVER SLEEPS: A RANDALL & CARVER MYSTERY

RANDALL & CARVER MYSTERIES
BOOK 3

BLAIR HOWARD

Published Cleveland, TN 2025

ISBN-13: 979-8-9908529-9-0

Blair Howard Books

www.blairhowardbooks.com

blairhoward@blairhowardbooks.com

DEDICATION

To my beautiful daughter Mallory for whom the main character in this story is named.

PROLOGUE

THERE WAS NO MOON THAT NIGHT, JUST A WASH OF STARS scattered across the Tennessee sky like salt spilled on a black velvet blanket. A soft breeze rustled through the trees, nature's fingers playing across the leaves in the gentle rhythm of approaching autumn. In this remote corner of rural Tennessee, the darkness belonged to the crickets, to the occasional hoot of an owl, and to the secrets that only darkness could keep.

Terry Fisher moved quietly along the gravel road, his boots crunching softly with each step. The twenty-eight-year-old had the lean build of someone who worked with his hands, shoulders squared under a denim jacket despite the warm September evening. His dark hair fell into his eyes as he walked, head down, hands shoved deep in his pockets. The thin line of his mouth betrayed tension, the crease between his eyebrows showing he was lost in thought.

As the fence line for the Parsons farm appeared in the distance, Terry slowed his pace. He'd agreed to this meeting against his better judgment. It wasn't like him to be out this late, especially on a weeknight, and he didn't like it one bit, but the reply to his message had been insistent. *I understand. It needs to be tonight. You know where. Do not tell anyone.* And so here he was, walking the Tennessee back roads at eleven-thirty, the small flashlight in his pocket barely used, his eyes having adjusted to the darkness.

"I am... I'm getting out," he whispered to himself, rehearsing the words he'd say soon. "This is the last time, for sure. Tiffany and I are moving forward. Getting married. Starting clean. No arguments."

The old oak tree loomed ahead; its massive trunk silhouetted against the star-filled sky. It marked the corner of the Parsons' property, a natural landmark where the fence turned ninety degrees to follow the property line. It was also where the meeting was to take place, far from any roads, far from any homes, far from curious eyes and ears.

Terry checked his watch. It was 11:42 PM. He was early, but that was intentional. He wanted to arrive first, to have the psychological advantage of waiting rather than being waited for. It was a small thing, but tonight... Well, he knew he needed every advantage he could get.

He leaned against the oak tree and took a cigarette from his pocket. He rarely smoked anymore—Tiffany had asked him to quit—but he kept a few for moments of stress. This certainly qualified. The flame from his lighter briefly illuminated his face, the sharp planes of his cheekbones, the hint of stubble along his jaw, the tightness around his blue eyes.

"Last time," he muttered again, exhaling smoke into the night air. "Last time and I'm done."

The events of the past year flashed through his mind. It had started so innocently. A favor for a friend, he'd thought. Just look the other way, just hold something for a few hours, just make an introduction. But favors had a way of multiplying, of growing teeth, of becoming demands. And now he was in too deep, knowing too much about things he'd never wanted to be part of.

gunrunning wasn't what he'd imagined for his life. He'd grown up in this small town, had gone to the church youth group, had played football at the high school, had helped his mother with the groceries. He'd been the boy who walked old Mrs. Henderson's dog when her arthritis got bad. And now he was the man who helped move illegal firearms, who kept his mouth shut about shipments and buyers, who looked the other way when money changed hands.

All for what? The extra cash hadn't been worth it. The excitement had worn off quickly. The realization that he was breaking the law—serious federal laws—had settled in his stomach like a stone. And lately, the fear. The growing, gnawing fear that he was into something he couldn't escape.

But tonight, he would. Tonight, he would end it. He'd rehearsed what he would say, how he would say it firmly but without accusation, without threat. He wasn't going to the police. He wasn't going to talk. He just wanted out. He wanted to marry Tiffany, maybe start a family, be the man his father had raised him to be.

Terry checked his watch again. 11:58 PM. Almost time.

The sound came from behind him—a twig snapping almost imperceptibly over the nighttime chorus of insects. Terry turned, dropped his cigarette and ground it underfoot.

"You're early too," he said, squinting into the darkness, trying to make out the approaching figure. The silhouette was familiar in its movements, the way it approached with purpose but without hurry.

"Have you been waiting long?" The voice was measured, calm.

"Just a few minutes," Terry replied, straightening up from the tree. "Thanks for meeting me."

"No problem." The figure stopped several feet away, still

partially obscured by the shadows. "Something about you wanting out?"

Terry swallowed, his rehearsed speech suddenly forgotten. He nodded. "Yeah. I... I can't do this anymore. The guns, the money... I'm getting married in a few months. I need to be done with all this."

Silence stretched between them, punctuated only by the rhythmic chirping of crickets and the distant call of a night bird.

"Just like that?" The voice remained even, emotionless. "You think you can just walk away?"

"I'm not going to cause any trouble," Terry said quickly, holding up his hands. "I won't say anything to anyone. I just want to be done. Clean slate."

"After everything you've seen? Everything you know?" A small, humorless laugh. "That's not how it works, Terry."

A chill ran down Terry's spine that had nothing to do with the night air. "Look, I've been loyal," he said. "I've kept my mouth shut. I'm not asking for anything except to be left alone."

"And if I say no?"

Terry took a deep breath. "Then I'll leave town. Me and Tiffany. We'll start fresh somewhere else. No one needs to worry about me."

The figure took a step closer, the moonlight now catching the outline more clearly. "You know, I actually believe you, Terry. I believe you'd keep quiet."

Relief flooded through Terry. "Then we're good? I'm out?"

"The problem isn't what you'd do," the voice continued, as if he hadn't spoken. "It's what you represent. If you walk away, others might think they can too. And then what? My whole operation falls apart because Terry Fisher wanted to play house with his girlfriend?"

"That's not—"

"You made commitments," the voice hardened. "You took money. You knew what you were getting into."

Terry shook his head, desperation creeping into his voice. "I didn't, though. Not really. It got bigger than I expected. More dangerous."

"And that's supposed to be my problem?"

"Please," Terry took a step forward. "I'm begging you. I'll do one last job if that helps. Whatever you need. But after that, I'm done."

The silence that followed was heavier than before, laden with unspoken threats and calculations.

"One last job," the figure finally said. The voice sounded thoughtful.

Hope bloomed in Terry's chest. "Yes. Anything."

"And then we never see each other again."

"Exactly," Terry nodded eagerly. "Clean break."

"Turn around."

Terry blinked, confused. "What?"

"Turn around. Look at the view. I want to discuss what this last job would entail, and I think better when I'm looking at the stars."

It was an odd request, but Terry was too relieved to question it. He turned, facing away from the figure, looking out over the Parsons' property. The field stretched before him, a sea of tall grass silvered by starlight, rolling gently toward the tree line in the distance.

"Beautiful, isn't it?" the voice said, now just behind him.

"Yeah," Terry agreed, shoulders relaxing slightly. "Peaceful."

"Do you know what I've learned in this business, Terry?" The voice was calm, almost philosophical. "I've learned that peace is an illusion. There's always trouble brewing under the surface. Always someone wanting more than they deserve."

Terry started to turn. "I don't—"

"Don't move," the voice commanded sharply. "Just listen."

Terry froze, a new fear creeping up his spine.

"I trusted you," the voice continued, now with an edge of disappointment. "I brought you in. Made you part of something bigger than this backwater town could ever offer you. And this is how you repay me? By trying to walk away?"

"I told you, I won't—"

"Quiet." The word was delivered without heat, but with absolute authority. "I know what you think. That you're different. Special. That the rules don't apply to you."

Terry felt the presence move closer, just inches behind him now. "Please," he whispered. "I just want—"

"What you want doesn't matter anymore, Terry. What matters is the message."

The first shot came without further warning, a muffled crack that seemed impossibly loud in the quiet night. The bullet entered the back of Terry's skull with surgical precision, stealing his words, his thoughts, his future with Tiffany. Before his body could crumple, a second shot followed the first, a redundancy born of professionalism rather than passion.

Terry Fisher fell forward, face first into the tall grass of the Parsons' farm. No last words, no dramatic clutching at life, just a sudden, brutal transition from existence to absence.

The figure stood over the body for a long moment, breathing steadily, no hint of panic or regret. The gun, still warm, disappeared into a pocket. Hands reached down, checking for a pulse more out of habit than necessity. Finding none, the figure straightened and surveyed the scene with clinical detachment.

Terry Fisher lay dead in the gentle slope of the field, his blood soaking into the earth, his body already beginning to cool under the indifferent stars. The crickets, momentarily silenced by the gunshots, gradually resumed their chorus.

The killer turned and walked away unhurriedly, footsteps

deliberate and careful, leaving no trail, no evidence, nothing but a cooling body in a farmer's field. The night swallowed the retreating figure, darkness embracing darkness, secrets kept in the shadows where they belonged.

By morning, dew would settle on Terry's still form. By midday, a teenage boy cutting across the field would discover him and make the panicked call to the sheriff's office. By evening, the rumors would begin—drugs, gambling debts, love triangles—the small town trying to make sense of the senselessness.

But for now, in the deep of night, there was only silence, only stars, only the soft footsteps of someone walking away from murder, already calculating the next move in a game where the taking of human lives was merely collateral damage.

1

MALLORY CARVER SUPPRESSED A YAWN AS SHE FLIPPED THROUGH yet another bridal magazine, her finger tracing over glossy images of wedding dresses that, after three hours, all seemed to blend together. She sighed, shook her head, and watched the dust motes dancing in the late afternoon sunlight streaming in through Jen's bay windows, highlighting the scattered wedding paraphernalia that had gradually consumed her sister's living room. Across from her, Jen sat at the table, meticulously organizing swatches of fabric and photos of floral arrangements into a binder that had grown to the size of a small dictionary.

The coffee table between them had disappeared beneath layers of wedding magazines, cake design options, and invitation samples. Mallory's eyes burned slightly from the endless parade of white, cream, and ivory, each shade supposedly distinct but looking maddeningly similar after hours of scrutiny.

"What about this one?" Jen asked, rotating a magazine toward Mallory. "The lace detail on the sleeves would complement your figure beautifully." She tapped a manicured nail against the page, her wedding ring catching the light. Jen, at forty-four, had been married to Jared for nearly twenty-four years, and sometimes Mallory wondered if her sister was more excited about this wedding than she was.

Mallory tilted her head, studying the dress. It was elegant—maybe a bit too elegant for the outdoor ceremony she and Tucker had agreed on. The intricate beadwork and cathedral-length train seemed better suited to a grand church with stained glass windows than the botanical garden venue they'd secured.

"It's pretty, but isn't it a little formal for a garden wedding?" she asked, trying to picture herself navigating grass and gravel in something that elaborate. "I'd probably trip over that train and face-plant into the wedding cake."

Jen rolled her eyes. "You can never be too formal on your wedding day, Mal. Besides, I thought you wanted the dress to be the one extravagant element." She closed one magazine, immediately opened another, and flipped to a dog-eared page. "And there are ways to bustle the train for the reception. Jackie could help with that—she's got nimble fingers."

Mallory smiled at the mention of her sixteen-year-old niece. "Jackie would probably add hidden pockets for my lock picks and pepper spray."

"Don't even joke about that," Jen said, but her lips twitched. "That girl has been obsessed with your cases ever since..." she trailed off, the unspoken reference to Julie's murder hanging in the air between them.

Mallory reached across the table to squeeze her sister's hand. It had been nearly three years since they'd solved her older niece's murder, but the pain was still raw for all of them. Julie would have been almost twenty-four now, probably finishing graduate school, perhaps even planning her own wedding.

Jen blinked rapidly and refocused on the magazine. "Anyway, back to your dress. I do like the sweetheart neckline on this one, but maybe with a simpler skirt? What d'you think?"

"Yes... but—" Mallory's phone vibrated on the coffee table,

the screen lighting up with a notification, and she reached for it instinctively. Work had been hectic lately, with three active surveillance cases keeping her and Tucker occupied from dawn until well past dusk most days.

"Don't you dare," Jen warned, slapping her hand away with a fabric swatch. "We agreed. Two hours of uninterrupted wedding planning." Her tone was light, but Mallory could hear the underlying frustration. This wasn't the first time they'd tried to nail down wedding details, only for Mallory to get distracted by work.

"It's been three hours," Mallory countered, checking her watch. "And I'm pretty sure my brain will leak out of my ears if I look at one more variation of white fabric."

She rubbed her temples; a dull headache had been building for the past hour. While she loved her sister dearly, Jen's approach to wedding planning was exhaustingly thorough. No detail was too small to dissect, no option too remote to consider.

Jen sighed dramatically, tucking a strand of hair behind her ear. At forty-four, Jen Romero was still strikingly beautiful, with only the faintest lines around her eyes betraying the twelve-year age gap between the sisters. Her dark hair was expertly high-lighted, her clothes tastefully expensive, her home immaculately decorated—everything about Jen screamed polished perfection.

Beside her, Mallory often felt like the perpetual kid sister—the "accident" their parents had had in their forties, the family wild card who'd never quite fit the mold. Where Jen was elegant and traditional, Mallory was practical and unconventional. Where Jen had married young and built a picture-perfect family life, Mallory had bounced between relationships and careers before finding her calling as a private investigator.

"Therefore, you have to make decisions now, Mal," Jen insisted, her voice taking on the patient tone she typically reserved for her teenage daughter. "The wedding is only six months away. Vendors need deposits. Dresses need alterations. Invitations need to be ordered. Do you have any idea how quickly time will fly?"

"Six months is an eternity," Mallory argued, stretching her arms above her head until her shoulders popped satisfyingly. She'd spent too many hours sitting still. "Tucker and I could solve a dozen cases in that time. Remember the Wilkins inheritance fraud? We cracked that one in three days."

"Speaking of Tucker," Jen said, flipping to another section of her wedding binder, "has he made any decisions on his tux yet? The groomsmen need to coordinate, and Jared will need time for alterations." She pulled out a color-coded spreadsheet of timeline milestones that made Mallory's eyes cross.

"We haven't even confirmed who the groomsmen are yet," Mallory reminded her. "Besides, Tucker thinks the entire wedding planning process is an elaborate form of torture specifically designed to break hardened criminals. He keeps saying we should just elope."

"He wouldn't," Jen gasped, clutching her wedding binder to her chest as if it were a shield against such blasphemy. Her expression of genuine horror made Mallory laugh.

"Relax," she said, reaching for her water glass. "He's not serious. Well, mostly not serious." She paused, considering. "Okay, he's about sixty percent serious, but I've vetoed the idea. He'll come around."

Mallory had known from the beginning that Tucker wasn't the type to dream about big weddings. At thirty-four, he'd been a dedicated bachelor before they'd met, focused entirely on his career. He approached wedding planning the same way he approached surveillance—as a necessary but tedious task to be endured rather than enjoyed.

"What's his issue, anyway?" Jen asked, making a note in her

binder. "I thought men just had to show up in a tux and say 'I do.' It's not like he's the one trying on fifty dresses."

"He's not thrilled about the outdoor venue," Mallory admitted, remembering Tucker's face when they'd toured the botanical gardens. He'd looked like a man marching to his doom.

"What's wrong with the garden? It's gorgeous in spring. Those cherry blossoms will be perfect for photos."

"He says it's too weather dependent," Mallory replied. "What if it rains? What if there's a freak heat wave? What if a swarm of locusts descends upon our nuptials?" Mallory deepened her voice in a surprisingly accurate impression of Tucker's baritone, complete with his characteristic eyebrow raise. "Mallory, statistical analysis of Chattanooga springtime shows a thirty-two percent chance of precipitation during our designated time window."

Jen laughed despite herself, setting down her pen. "Tucker Randall, afraid of a little rain," she chuckled, shaking her head. "The man who chased down that armed robber is worried about getting his hair wet? I don't believe it."

The memory of that case flashed through Mallory's mind—Tucker sprinting through a crowded farmer's market, vaulting over a produce stand to tackle a suspect who'd pulled a gun. He'd ended up with a black eye and a sprained wrist, but the embezzler had been arrested, and their client's stolen retirement funds recovered. It had been over two years ago, their third case together, before their professional partnership had evolved into something more personal.

"It's not the rain he's worried about. It's the unpredictability," Mallory explained, her voice softening with affection. "You know how he is. He likes to control variables, to plan for every contingency. A man who keeps three backup weapons and memorizes the floor plan of every building he enters doesn't like leaving things to chance."

Tucker's methodical nature was what made him such an excellent investigator—and sometimes such a challenging partner. Where Mallory followed hunches and intuition, Tucker relied on evidence and logic. Their different approaches had led to more than a few heated arguments, but they'd also helped them solve cases that had baffled others.

"Most PI's do," Jen nodded sagely, as if she hadn't learned everything she knew about private investigators from true crime podcasts and her sister's stories. She had eagerly devoured every detail of Mallory's cases since she'd joined Tucker's agency, asking questions that ranged from insightful to amusingly naïve.

"Is it always like on TV?" she'd asked once. "Do you wear disguises and have car chases?" The reality—hours of monotonous surveillance, mind-numbing paperwork, and witnesses who misremembered crucial details—was far less glamorous than fictional depictions, but occasionally they did get cases that rivaled anything on screen.

Mallory's phone buzzed again on the coffee table, the screen lighting up with another notification. An email had come through to their business account—the one that forwarded to both her and Tucker's phones. Usually, it was just routine inquiries: potential clients asking about rates, current clients requesting updates, occasionally spam that made it through the filters.

"Mallory," Jen warned, her tone that of a kindergarten teacher catching a student reaching for cookies before lunch.

"Just a quick peek," Mallory promised, already reaching for the phone. She'd developed the ability to quickly triage communications during her years working on cases, separating urgent matters from those that could wait. "It could be important. Maybe the Hendersons have new information about their neighbor's suspicious late-night activities."

"The murderers will still be there tomorrow," Jen said, her

tone half-joking, half-exasperated. She tapped her watch meaningfully. "Your wedding dress decisions won't wait. The boutique needs six months for custom orders, and even off-the-rack options need alterations."

But Mallory was already skimming the email, her posture straightening instinctively as she read. The subject line had caught her attention immediately: "Unsolved Murder - My Brother Deserves Justice."

She'd seen plenty of cold case inquiries over the years. Most were rambling, fueled by grief that hadn't faded with time, often lacking crucial details. This one was different. The message was from someone named Gary Fisher, detailing the unsolved murder of his brother Terry eleven years earlier. Terry had been found on a farmer's property, shot twice in the back of the head execution-style. No arrests had ever been made, no suspects had ever been named publicly.

What struck Mallory was the methodical organization of the email. It was huge. Gary Fisher had included dates, times, locations, names of the original investigating officers. He'd attached a PDF timeline of events surrounding the murder, along with scanned newspaper clippings and what appeared to be copies of the initial police statements from several witnesses. This wasn't just a grieving relative reaching out in desperation—this was someone who had been conducting his own investigation for years.

"Jen, listen to this," Mallory said, reading aloud from the email. "My parents are elderly and in declining health. My father has only a few months to live. All they want to know before they pass is who killed their son and why. The local police have given up. You guys are my last hope for justice."

The urgency resonated with Mallory. She remembered all too well the agonizing weeks when Julie had first disappeared, the desperate need for answers that had consumed their family.

"That's sad," Jen conceded, her expression softening, "but you get emails like this all the time, don't you? People whose cases have gone cold, looking for whatever help they can find."

"Not like this," Mallory said, continuing to scroll through Gary's message. She skimmed the detailed timeline he'd created, noting how each event was documented. He'd listed every person his brother Terry had contact with during the days before his death, every location he'd visited, even the weather conditions on the day the body was found.

"So what makes this one different?" Jen asked, closing her wedding binder with a resigned sigh, clearly sensing that their planning session was effectively over.

Mallory wasn't entirely sure she could articulate it. Part of it was the thoroughness of Gary's documentation, part of it was the looming deadline of his parents' failing health, but there was something else—a pattern in the details that tickled the back of her mind, though she couldn't quite place it yet.

"I don't know exactly," she admitted, biting her lower lip as she continued to read. "But there's something about this case... It feels... different, important. The execution-style killing, the rural setting, the complete lack of progress after eleven years. And the parents who might die without ever knowing who killed their son."

She scrolled through more of the attached documents, finding a photograph of Terry Fisher—a young man with an easy smile, dark hair falling over bright eyes, his arm slung around a woman Mallory assumed was his fiancée. According to Gary's notes, Terry had been planning to get married just three months after he was killed.

"I need to show this to Tucker," she said, already dialing his number. The wedding magazines lay forgotten on the coffee table as Mallory began pacing across Jen's living room, phone pressed to her ear.

Tucker answered on the third ring, his voice carrying that slightly guarded tone he used when expecting wedding-related questions. "Please tell me this is about dinner plans and not flower arrangements."

"Check your email," Mallory said without preamble, too focused to be amused by his wariness. "The business account. Something just came in from a Gary Fisher about his brother's murder."

"Give me a second," Tucker replied, and she could hear the faint clicking of his keyboard through the phone. Tucker would be sitting at his desk in their small home office, probably reviewing surveillance photos or drafting a client report. He was meticulous about documentation, keeping their case files organized with a precision that sometimes bordered on obsessive.

Jen caught Mallory's eye across the room and mouthed, "Wedding plans?" with an exaggerated pout, gesturing to the abandoned magazines.

Mallory covered the phone with her hand. "Tomorrow, I promise. Dinner and full wedding focus." She knew she was making a promise she might not keep, but in the moment, she meant it.

"You've got that look in your eyes," Jen sighed, gathering up some of the scattered fabric swatches. "The one that means you're about to disappear into a case for weeks and forget that the rest of the world exists."

Mallory couldn't argue with that. The familiar buzz of anticipation was already coursing through her veins, the same feeling she got at the start of every challenging case. She was like a bloodhound catching a scent—once she had it, she couldn't let go until she'd followed it to its source.

"I'm reading it now," Tucker's voice came through the phone, pulling her attention back. "Cold case, rural area, execution-style killing..." She could practically see him frowning as he analyzed the information. "Sounds like a long shot, Mal. These rural jurisdictions don't always preserve evidence properly, witnesses disappear or die, documentation gets spotty."

"Duckwood isn't exactly rural, Tucker, and... His parents are dying," Mallory pressed, pacing more quickly now. "His father only has months left to live. Don't they deserve answers before it's too late?" She walked to the window, looking out at Jen's backyard, thinking of the Fisher family living with an open wound for eleven years.

There was a moment of silence. Tucker wasn't one to make hasty decisions, especially when it came to taking on new cases. She could imagine him mentally reviewing their current work-load, calculating billable hours, assessing their resources.

"You know how difficult these cold cases can be," he finally said, his tone cautious. "Small-town police departments with limited resources, evidence that's probably been mishandled or lost by now, witnesses whose memories have faded or who've moved away—"

"So we don't even try?" Mallory countered, cutting him off, her voice rising slightly, passion creeping in. "We've solved cases with less to go on. Remember the Caldwell fraud? All we had were bank statements from six years ago and a hunch."

"That was different," Tucker said, but she could hear the slight waver in his voice. Despite his rational, methodical approach to cases, Tucker was at heart a man driven by justice. It was why he'd left the FBI after a case went wrong—not because he'd stopped caring, but because he cared too much.

"We should drive out there," Mallory said before he could fully formulate his objections. "Meet with Gary Fisher in person, get a feel for the situation on the ground. If it's a dead end, we'll know quickly enough."

"Mal, we've got three active cases here in Chattanooga, plus all this wedding stuff—" Tucker's voice held a note of exasperation now.

"The wedding isn't for six months," she interrupted, ignoring Jen's dramatic gasp from across the room. "And those other cases are just surveillance jobs. They can wait a day or two." She knew she was pushing, perhaps too hard, but there was something about this case that was pulling at her.

The silence on the line told her Tucker was wavering. She knew better than to push harder; after nearly three years together, she'd learned when to let him come to a decision on his own. Tucker didn't respond well to pressure, but he did respond to reason and to his own moral compass, which invariably pointed toward helping those in need.

Finally, she heard him sigh, a sound that signaled surrender. "Fine. I'll reach out and set up a meeting. But we're not committing to anything yet, understood? This is just a preliminary reconnaissance."

"Understood," Mallory agreed, a smile spreading across her face as she turned back to face her sister. "Let me know when you've arranged it."

She ended the call and tucked her phone into her pocket, already mentally packing for their trip. Jen was staring at her with a mixture of annoyance and affection, arms crossed over her chest.

"There goes our wedding planning," Jen said, but there was no real anger in her voice. After decades of Mallory's unpredictable nature, Jen had developed a tolerant resignation to her younger sister's sudden changes of direction.

"Just for... a few days. Maybe only one," Mallory promised, gathering her purse from the side table. The wedding magazines could stay; she'd pick them up next time. "Besides, you've already done most of the work. I just need to pick a dress and show up, right?"

"If only it were that simple," Jen muttered, but she stood to walk Mallory to the door. "Just promise me one thing?"

"What's that?" Mallory asked, slinging her bag over her shoulder.

"Try not to get shot this time? Jackie's still traumatized from your last big case, and I don't want to have to explain to Mom and Dad why their youngest daughter has a new bullet hole."

Mallory thought of her sixteen-year-old niece, who had developed a fascination with true crime after Mallory and Tucker had solved the murder of her older sister Julie the previous year. Jackie had gone from a typical teenager obsessed with social media to someone who listened to true crime podcasts and asked unsettlingly specific questions about investigative techniques. Trauma manifested in strange ways sometimes.

"I'll do my best," Mallory said, giving her sister a quick hug. "No promises, though. You know how these things go."

"That's what worries me," Jen replied, her smile not quite reaching her eyes. "Just... be careful. And maybe check in more than once a week this time?"

"I will," Mallory promised, meaning it. Three years before, during the investigation into Julie's disappearance and murder, she'd gotten so absorbed in the case that she'd barely communicated with her family. Looking back, she regretted not being more present for Jen during that horrific time.

"Oh, and would you mind looking after Annie while I'm gone?" she asked. Annie was her seven-year-old Border Collie.

"You know I will," Jen replied. "Drop her off whenever you like."

"Thanks, sis. I..." She was going to say I owe you one, but she owed her many more than one, so she simply turned, smiled, and hugged her, then pivoted and walked away, leaving her sister staring after her.

2

AS SHE WALKED TO HER CAR, MALLORY COULD ALREADY FEEL HER mind shifting into investigative mode. Already, she was mentally cataloging the details from Gary's email. Two shots to the back of the head. Execution-style. A rural setting. An investigation that had apparently stalled almost immediately. A family still seeking answers after more than a decade.

She couldn't explain exactly why this particular case had caught her attention the way it had. They received literally dozens of cold case inquiries each month, and very rarely did one grab her the way this one had. Perhaps it was the methodical way Gary had presented the information, or the urgency of his parents' failing health. Or perhaps it was simply that Terry Fisher had been engaged to be married when he was killed—a young man on the cusp of starting his life with someone he loved, only to have it all ripped away.

Whatever it was, her instincts rarely led her astray. Tucker often teased her about her "hunches," but even he had learned to trust her intuition. *There's something here*, she thought, *something worth pursuing. I can feel it in my bones.*

Her phone buzzed with a text from Tucker: *Meeting with*

Gary Fisher tomorrow at 11 AM. It's a 90-minute drive. Pack overnight. I'll pick you up at 9 AM.

Mallory smiled to herself as she slid into the driver's seat of her Honda CRV.

Tucker might pretend to be reluctant, she thought, *but he's already planning ahead, already assuming we'll need more than a day to assess the situation.*

And that was the thing about Tucker; once he committed to something, he did it thoroughly. No half measures, no cutting corners.

And that was the thing about their partnership. It was personal and professional. They balanced each other perfectly. Where she was intuitive, he was analytical. Where she rushed in, he proceeded with caution. Where she followed her heart, he followed the evidence. She provided the intuitive leaps, the passionate pursuits; he contributed the methodical planning, the careful consideration. They pushed each other, challenged each other, and ultimately made each other better investigators.

Together, they solved cases that neither could crack by themselves.

This one would be no different. Someone had killed Terry Fisher eleven years ago, and his family deserved to know why. If the local police couldn't or wouldn't provide those answers, then Mallory and Tucker would just have to do it themselves.

As she drove home to pack, Mallory felt that familiar tingling sensation at the base of her skull, the one that told her they were about to uncover something big. Something dangerous. The feeling she'd had three years before when she and Tucker had gone after Julie's killer, and a dozen times since. She shook her head and smiled as she remembered that first meeting, how it almost never happened, and how he insisted he worked alone. Persuading him to let her tag along hadn't been easy. *But look where we are now,* she thought.

Her phone rang again, breaking into her thoughts. She answered through the car's Bluetooth system. It was Tucker.

"I need you to download everything Gary Fisher attached to his email," he said without preamble. "There's a lot to go through before tomorrow, and I want us both up to speed before we meet him."

"You got it," she replied, making a mental note to stop for coffee on the way home. It would be a late night of research. "Anything jump out at you?" she asked.

Tucker was silent for a moment, and she could almost see him organizing his thoughts, choosing his words carefully as he always did. "Maybe," he replied. "The victim's girlfriend at the time is now married to his cousin. That's an interesting development. And the local police chief, Nate Winson; his name appears in some online forum posts speculating about corruption. Nothing concrete, but it's worth looking into."

"I saw that too," Mallory said, feeling a surge of excitement. "And there's the murder itself, the execution style—two shots to the back of the head. That's smacks of a professional hit, don't you think?"

"Possibly," Tucker replied. "Or maybe it was made to look that way. Rural Tennessee has plenty of hunters, so familiarity with firearms is common. Don't jump to conclusions about hitmen or organized crime just yet."

Mallory laughed. "You know me too well."

"Indeed, I do," he agreed, his voice warming slightly. "That's why I already called the hotel in Duckwood and booked us a room for at least three nights. Two beds," he added quickly. "For propriety's sake, since we're not married yet."

The formality made her smile. Despite their engagement and the fact that they almost lived together, Tucker maintained certain old-fashioned sensibilities when they were working. "Always the gentleman," she joked.

"Professional," he corrected. "We're representing the agency. I don't want small-town gossip interfering with our investigation."

"Fair enough," she conceded, turning onto her street. "What else did you find in Gary's materials?"

"There's a mention of some local Baptist church that Terry attended regularly. The pastor there might be worth talking to if he's still around after eleven years."

"Good thinking," Mallory said as she pulled into her driveway. "Churches are information hubs in small towns. People talk to their pastors, share things they wouldn't tell police."

"Exactly. There's also—" Tucker paused, and she heard keyboard clicks in the background. "Hold on, I just got another email from Gary. He's sending more documents. Old newspaper clippings about the case, some photocopied police statements... Mallory, this guy has been working this case for years."

"I told you there was something here," she said, unable to keep the satisfaction from her voice.

"Let's not get ahead of ourselves," Tucker cautioned. "Having a lot of documents doesn't mean they contain a lot of useful information. For all we know, Gary's spent a decade compiling irrelevant details."

"We'll find out tomorrow," Mallory said, gathering her purse as she parked. "I'm home now. I'll go through everything tonight."

"I'll call you in the morning at seven sharp and pick you up at nine

"I'll be ready. And Tucker?"

"Yeah?"

"Thanks for taking this seriously. I know we're busy, but... I just have a feeling about this one."

There was a pause on the line. "Your feelings have panned

out before," he admitted grudgingly. "Just... keep an open mind. Don't get tunnel vision on any one theory."

"I promise," she said. "See you at nine. Love you."

"Love you, too," he replied.

Mallory ended the call and sat in her car for a moment, watching the last rays of afternoon sunlight filter through the trees in her front yard. Her thoughts drifted to Terry Fisher, a young man whose life had been violently cut short eleven years ago, whose parents were now dying without answers, whose brother hadn't stopped searching for justice.

Her phone buzzed with a text from Jen: "Since we didn't decide on a dress today, I'm making an appointment at Bridal Elegance for next week. Non-negotiable."

Mallory smiled and texted back: "Deal. And I'll actually show up this time."

Setting her phone on the passenger seat, she reached into the glove compartment and pulled out a small notebook—an old-fashioned habit in a digital age, but one that had served her well. On a fresh page, she wrote "TERRY FISHER CASE" and underlined it twice.

Below that, she jotted her initial questions:

· Why execution style? Professional hit or made to look that way?

· Connection to other victims?

· Nate Winson - corrupt cop or victim of rumors?

· Tiffany (ex-fiancée) - now married to the victim's cousin. Suspicious timing?

· Local church connection - what did Terry confide in his pastor?

· Why has the case gone cold for 11 years despite Gary's efforts?

She tapped her pen against the page, then added one more question:

· Who stands to benefit from Terry Fisher's death? Follow the money/motive.

It wasn't much to go on, but it was a start. Tomorrow they would meet with Gary, see the actual town where the murder took place, begin to get a feel for the cast of characters in this long-dormant mystery. And, if Tucker was right, it would probably lead nowhere—just another cold case destined to remain unsolved, another family left without closure.

But if Mallory's instincts were correct, they were about to uncover something that had been deliberately buried for over a decade. Something dangerous enough that someone had been willing to kill to keep it hidden.

She closed the notebook and stepped out of her car. She had packing to do, research to review, sleep to grab before their morning departure. Tucker would arrive exactly at nine—not eight-fifty-nine, not one minute after nine—and he'd expect her to be ready to go.

That was one more thing about their partnership she had come to appreciate. They kept each other accountable, balanced each other's strengths and weaknesses. His methodical nature tempered her impulsivity; her intuition complemented his logic.

Together, they made a formidable team. And starting tomorrow, they would put that partnership to work on behalf of a family that had waited far too long for answers.

As she turned the key in her front door, Mallory felt that familiar surge of anticipation that came with starting a new case. The late nights, the dead ends, the breakthrough moments, the rush of finally piecing together a puzzle that others had abandoned. And that was what she lived for. Not wedding dresses or flower arrangements, but the pursuit of truth, however uncomfortable or dangerous it might be.

She was met enthusiastically by Annie, her energetic border collie.

"Hello, girlfriend," she said. "Have you been a good girl? I have a surprise for you. You're going to visit your aunt and uncle for a few days. Won't that be nice? Come on, let's go potty and then I'll give you some dinner."

That done, she grabbed a soft drink from the fridge, sat down at the table, took her laptop from her bag, opened it, and got to work.

Forty-five minutes later, she gave it up, pushed the laptop away, folded her arms, frowned, then muttered, "This isn't working. We should be doing this together."

3

TUCKER RANDALL LEANED BACK IN HIS OFFICE CHAIR, STRETCHING his neck from side to side as he scrolled through the surveillance photos on his computer screen. Three hours of watching the Henderson property had yielded exactly two usable images of their neighbor's suspicious late-night activities. The rest were just shadows and normal neighborhood comings and goings. Nothing that would definitively prove the illegal subletting that Mrs. Henderson suspected.

The office—an addition to the left side of his home—was quiet this late in the afternoon, just the hum of the air conditioning and the occasional car passing on the street outside. Tucker preferred it that way—no distractions, no interruptions, just him and the evidence. It wasn't fancy, but it was functional, and most importantly, affordable.

The walls were lined with filing cabinets—Tucker's insistence, despite Mallory's argument that everything should be digital now. He'd compromised by maintaining both paper and electronic records. Technology failed; paper endured. It was a lesson he'd learned the hard way during his FBI days when a server crash had temporarily wiped out months of case files.

Tucker clicked through several more photos, making notes in his precise, squared-off handwriting that Mallory often teased him about. "It's like a robot is writing in hieroglyphics," she'd said once, peering over his shoulder at a case report. He'd retorted that at least his notes were legible, unlike her hasty scrawl that sometimes even she couldn't decipher later.

The memory made him smile slightly. For all their differences in approach, he and Mallory made an effective team. Her intuitive leaps sometimes led them down rabbit holes, but just as often, they cracked cases wide open. His methodical process ensured they didn't miss crucial details along the way.

When his phone rang again, Tucker glanced at the screen and felt a twinge of apprehension when he saw Mallory's name. She'd been wedding planning with her sister Jen, which meant the call likely involved flower arrangements, color schemes, or some other detail he was supposed to have an opinion on but genuinely didn't.

He took a deep breath and answered. "Please tell me this is about dinner plans and not flower arrangements."

"Check your email," Mallory said immediately, her voice carrying that distinct tone of excitement he recognized from the start of promising cases. "The business account. Something just came in from a Gary Fisher about his brother's murder."

Tucker sat up straighter, her enthusiasm momentarily contagious. He clicked over to their email, finding the message already at the top of their inbox. The subject line was direct: "Unsolved Murder - My Brother Deserves Justice."

"Give me a second," he said, opening the email and scanning the contents. They received plenty of cold case inquiries—enough that he'd created a standardized response for the ones they couldn't take on, which was most of them. But even at first glance, this one seemed more substantive than most.

The email was methodically organized, with clearly delineated sections for background, evidence, witness statements, and investigation notes. The writer, Gary Fisher, had included several attachments: a PDF timeline, scanned newspaper articles, and what appeared to be copies of police reports. Tucker's investigator instincts perked up at the thoroughness, even as his practical side noted the challenges inherent in such cases.

The basics were straightforward enough. Terry Fisher, twenty-eight years old, found shot execution-style on a farmer's property eleven years ago. No arrests, no named suspects, no apparent motive. The local police investigation had gone nowhere. Now the victim's parents were elderly and ill, seeking closure before they passed.

Mallory was already pushing for them to take the case, her voice growing more animated as she described the details he was still reading.

"I'm reading it now," Tucker said, tempering his response. "Cold case, rural area, execution-style killing..." He frowned as he scrolled through the attached timeline. "Sounds like a long shot, Mal. These rural jurisdictions don't always preserve evidence properly, witnesses disappear or die, documentation gets spotty."

"His parents are dying," Mallory pressed, the passion in her voice unmistakable. "His father only has months left to live. Don't they deserve answers before it's too late?"

Tucker sighed internally. Mallory's compassion was one of the things he admired most about her, but it sometimes clouded her professional judgment. He shook his head. Eleven years was a long time. Evidence degraded. Memories faded. Witnesses moved away or died. And rural police departments often lacked the resources and expertise to properly maintain case files for that long.

"You know how difficult these rural cold cases can be," he reminded her. "Small-town police departments with limited resources, evidence that's probably been mishandled or lost by now, witnesses whose memories have faded or who've moved away..."

"So we don't even try?" Mallory countered, her voice rising slightly. "We've solved cases with less to go on. Remember the Caldwell fraud? All we had were bank statements from six years ago and a hunch."

"That was different," Tucker said automatically, though he knew she had a point. The Caldwell case had seemed impossible until Mallory had spotted a pattern in the bank records that everyone else had missed. But financial fraud cases left paper trails; murders often didn't.

Tucker ran a hand through his short black hair, mentally reviewing their current caseload. Three active surveillance cases, all relatively straightforward. The Hendersons, worried about their neighbor illegally subletting. The Martins, suspecting their business partner of embezzlement. The Davidson divorce, where the husband was allegedly hiding assets. None were particularly time-sensitive or complex.

"We should drive out there," Mallory suggested, interrupting his thoughts. "Meet with Gary Fisher in person, get a feel for the situation on the ground. If it's a dead end, we'll know quickly enough."

That was actually a reasonable approach, Tucker had to admit. An initial assessment wouldn't commit them to taking the case, but it would give them enough information to make an informed decision.

"Mal, we've got three active cases here in Chattanooga, plus all this wedding stuff—" he began, more as a token protest than a genuine objection.

"The wedding isn't for six months," she interrupted, dismissing his concern. "And those other cases are just surveillance jobs. They can wait a day or two."

Tucker glanced at his calendar. She wasn't wrong. The surveillance cases could be paused briefly without issue. And a part of him was intrigued by the methodical way Gary Fisher had compiled his brother's case information. It suggested a careful, detail-oriented person—the kind of client Tucker preferred to work with.

He was also aware that Mallory's interest in this particular case likely stemmed partly from her own family's experience with her niece Julie's murder. The Fisher parents' desire for closure before they died resonated with her on a personal level.

After a moment's consideration, Tucker made his decision. "Fine. I'll reach out to set up a meeting. But we're not committing to anything yet, understood? This is just a preliminary reconnaissance."

"Understood," Mallory agreed, the smile clear in her voice. "Let me know when you've arranged it."

As soon as they ended the call, Tucker opened a new email to Gary Fisher, introducing himself and Mallory as investigators interested in discussing his brother's case. He suggested meeting the following day at 11 AM, noting they would drive from Chattanooga to—he checked the address—Duckwood, a small town about ninety minutes away in rural Tennessee.

The response came less than five minutes later. Gary was available and eager to meet. He provided his home address and phone number, along with effusive thanks for their interest.

Tucker texted Mallory with the details, and then he did a search for hotels in Duckwood, found one he liked and booked a room for three nights.

With the logistics handled, Tucker returned to the Fisher case materials, methodically working through each document. The execution-style killing—two shots to the back of the head—suggested either a professional hit or someone trying to make it look like one. The lack of robbery or sexual assault ruled out certain common motives. The body had been left where it fell, not hidden or moved, which indicated either confidence or panic on the killer's part.

The victim, Terry Fisher, had no criminal record. He'd worked as a contractor, was engaged to be married, attended church regularly. So, by all accounts, he was an ordinary young man in a small town. Nothing in his background screamed "murder victim." *So what the hell happened?* he wondered, *And why?*

Tucker opened an online forum thread Gary had linked in his email. Local speculation about the case ran rampant: wild theories from organized crime connections to satanic cult activity. Most of it was the usual nonsense that proliferated around unsolved murders, but one name kept appearing: Nate Winson, a local police officer who was now apparently the chief. Several anonymous posters suggested he might have deliberately mishandled evidence or even steered the investigation away from certain suspects.

This was potentially significant. Police corruption could explain why the case had gone unsolved despite the seemingly straightforward evidence. Tucker made a note to look into Winson's background and history with the department.

And then another detail caught his attention: Terry's fiancée, Tiffany Springer, had married his cousin Louis shortly after his death. *Hmm, interesting,* he thought. *That's an unusual development worth exploring.* Grief sometimes pushed people together, but the timing raised questions.

As Tucker continued reviewing the materials, his phone rang again. Seeing Mallory's name, he answered it.

"Hey, I just sent you everything Gary Fisher attached to his email," he said without waiting for her to speak. "There's a lot to go through before tomorrow. I want us both up to speed before we meet him."

A brief conversation followed about the case during which he told her of the arrangements he'd made in Duckwood and his plan to pick her up at nine in the morning.

After they ended the call, Tucker continued working through the case materials, creating a preliminary timeline and suspect list. As the sky outside his office window darkened, he finally stood, stretching his back and shoulders. He'd been hunched over his computer for hours, so absorbed in the Fisher case that he'd lost track of time.

The office was silent now, so Tucker grabbed his laptop and the notes he'd printed out, locked the front door, turned off the lights and made his way into the house. He would, he decided, continue reviewing the materials later.

As he walked through to the kitchen, he reflected on the investigation ahead and what it might entail. Cold cases were always challenging, but they had their own particular satisfaction when solved. Bringing closure to families, justice to victims long forgotten by everyone except those who loved them—it was work worth doing, even when the odds seemed long; too long, in some cases.

His phone buzzed with a text from Mallory: "I picked up dinner. Thai food. I'll be there in a few minutes."

Tucker smiled, typing back a quick affirmative. *Geez, does she never quit?* He shook his head. He knew just exactly what she was doing. She wanted to discuss the case and figured they could do it over dinner.

Tucker's mind continued working the Fisher case, turning over the sparse facts, looking for angles they could explore. He'd spent eight years with the FBI before resigning after the Marsha Cline case went so tragically wrong. Those years had taught him that even the most seemingly straightforward cases often contained hidden complexities. What might appear to be a simple rural murder could have tendrils extending in unexpected directions.

Mallory arrived a few minutes later to find the case materials spread across the surface of the table.

"Oh, that's nice," she said, her hazel eyes bright with the energy she always had at the beginning of a promising case.

"I thought I told you to go home and get some sleep," he said.

She shrugged. "Sleep? Seriously?" she joked. "It's only six-thirty. And besides, what was the point of me going over everything on my own and then have to discuss it all with you tomorrow? It's better we do it together, over dinner, don't you think?"

It was logical enough, and he could see she was full of enthusiasm, so, rather than argue with her, he nodded, got up and they both went to the kitchen.

He grabbed a couple of plates from the cupboard and they sat down at the table to eat.

"I've been cross-referencing the witness statements with the timeline Gary created," she said through a mouthful of food. She swallowed, then continued, "There are some inconsistencies in what people reported seeing the night Terry disappeared—"

"Can we give it a moment?" Tucker asked, cutting her off. "Let's eat, then we'll talk."

She pursed her lips, narrowed her eyes, stared across the table at him.

He stared stoically back at her, unyielding.

Finally, she gave it up, smiled, nodded, and said, "Oh hell, have it your way. You always do. And on that note, I'm not sure I want to marry you after all."

"Really," he replied. "I—"

"No, not really, you idiot," she snapped. "Now shut up and eat."

Thirty minutes later, coffee in hand, they were back,

standing at the dining room table, staring down at the dozens of printed sheets.

"What I was going to say when you so rudely cut me off," she began, "was that there are inconsistencies in what people reported seeing the night Terry disappeared, and..."

She paused, opened her briefcase, took out a sheet of paper, and said, "And look at this." She pushed a photocopy of a newspaper article toward him. "Three months after Terry's murder, there was another killing with the same MO. Corey Robar, a local contractor, found on the edge of a property about a mile from where they found Terry. Two shots to the back of the head."

"No kidding?" Tucker said, closing his laptop and examining the article with interest. "Connection to organized crime, perhaps? Or a serial killer, maybe?"

"That's what I'm thinking," Mallory said, holding up a map she'd printed. "Gary mentions this briefly in his notes but doesn't develop it. I found more details in some of the forum posts. And there's more." She paused, stared at him, waiting for a response.

"Well," he said. "Go on. What more?"

"Apparently, there have been four similar murders, all with the same MO, over the eleven years since Terry's death, all within a five-mile radius."

Tucker's eyebrows rose. He leaned back in his chair and stared at her. If what she said was true, it changed the entire complexion of the case.

"Five murders with the same MO, all unsolved, all in the same area?" he said, thoughtfully. "That can't be a coincidence."

"Exactly," Mallory nodded, her excitement palpable. "And get this; the local police never publicly connected the cases. Each one was treated as an isolated incident. Either they're incompetent, or..."

"Or someone's deliberately keeping them separate to hide the pattern," Tucker finished, his mind already calculating the implications. Multiple related murders increased the complexity but also provided more evidence, more potential witnesses, more opportunities to find connections.

They continued to discuss the case, Mallory's enthusiasm a counterpoint to Tucker's methodical analysis. By the time they finished, Tucker had a clearer picture of what they might be dealing with: either a serial killer who had somehow managed to operate undetected in a small community for over a decade, or a series of related murders connected to some local criminal enterprise that powerful people wanted to keep hidden.

Either way, it was potentially dangerous, and certainly more complex than the routine surveillance jobs that made up the bulk of their business lately.

"We should get some sleep," Tucker said finally, checking his watch. "It's after ten, and we need to leave by nine to make the meeting on time. You going to stay over?"

"I thought I might," she replied. "I dropped Annie off with Jen on the way here. I told her it might be a couple of days. That okay?"

Tucker made a face but didn't argue.

"Good," she said. "I'll set three alarms."

"Make it four," Tucker suggested, knowing her tendency to sleep through alarms. "And I'm thinking at least three days, so you might want to update Jen. I know it's only a little over ninety minutes away, but if we decide to take the case it might be prudent to stay in Duckwood for a while."

"Already packed," Mallory grinned, gesturing to a duffel bag by the door that Tucker hadn't noticed when she came in.

As they cleaned up, Tucker found himself reviewing mental checklists: equipment they should bring, questions to ask Gary, background information to verify. Cold cases required a different approach than fresh investigations. Evidence had to be reconstructed, witnesses re-interviewed with an understanding that memories had faded and changed. Time was both an obstacle and occasionally an ally, as people who'd kept secrets for years sometimes became willing to talk as they aged, as relationships changed, as old loyalties died.

Before turning in, Tucker made one more call—to Mike Preston, a former FBI colleague who now worked with the Tennessee Bureau of Investigation. He didn't expect Mike to answer this late, and he didn't, so Tucker left a brief message asking if the TBI had any information on the Fisher case or other unsolved murders in Duckwood over the past decade.

Mallory was already in bed when he joined her, but he could tell from her breathing that she wasn't asleep.

"Nervous about tomorrow?" he asked quietly in the darkness.

"Not nervous," she replied after a moment. "Just... I can't stop thinking about those parents. Waiting eleven years for answers about who killed their son, now running out of time."

Tucker reached for her hand beneath the covers. "We'll do our best," he promised. It was all he could offer; not certainty of success, but the assurance that they would pursue the truth with every tool and skill at their disposal.

"I know," Mallory murmured, squeezing his hand. "That's why I love you. You always do your best, even when the odds are long."

There was a moment of silence, then Mallory said, "Tucker!" Then rolled over, put her arm around him, then slid on top of him, and—

Tucker lay awake long after Mallory's breathing had deepened into sleep, his mind still working through the Fisher case. There was something about it that nagged at him; not just the details they'd uncovered so far, but some pattern or connection he couldn't quite grasp yet. Experience had taught him to trust that feeling, to let his subconscious mind process the information until the insight emerged.

As he finally drifted toward sleep, images from the case files floated through his mind: Terry Fisher's smiling face in a photograph with his fiancée, the stark police photos of his body in a rural field, and the newspaper clippings about subsequent murders. Something connected these deaths beyond the obvious similarities in method. Something that had remained hidden for eleven years.

Tomorrow they would begin unraveling that mystery, for the sake of parents who deserved to know the truth, and for a young man whose life had been cut short just as it was about to begin.

The last thought Tucker had before sleep claimed him was a simple promise, made to himself and to the victim he'd never met but whose cause he was already beginning to take as his own: *We'll find out who did this, Terry. No matter how long it takes.*

4

MALLORY CARVER BIT BACK A YAWN AS TUCKER'S SUV SPED along Highway 27 toward Duckwood. The clock on the dash read 9:32 AM.

"Tell me again why we needed to leave at the crack of dawn when our meeting isn't until eleven?" she asked, taking another sip from her travel mug.

Tucker kept his eyes on the road. "I texted Fisher. I changed the time to eleven-thirty. I want to take a look at the town," he replied. "I want time to get the lay of the land before meeting him. Besides, it's not the crack of dawn. I've been up since six."

"Of course you have," Mallory muttered, but there was affection in her tone. Tucker's sometimes mechanical, even fastidious, approach had saved their lives more than once.

As they drove, Mallory flipped through the case notes on her tablet. *Terry Fisher,* she thought, *twenty-eight years old, found shot execution-style on a farmer's property eleven years ago. No arrests, no suspects, a textbook cold case that had likely been mishandled from the start. Small-town police departments rarely had the resources or expertise for complex homicide investigations. Hah! So now what? Where do we begin?*

"So now what?" Mallory asked. "what's our strategy?" She set aside the tablet and turned her head to look at him. "Gary Fisher has been compiling information for years without cracking the case. What can we offer that local law enforcement couldn't?"

"Fresh eyes," Tucker replied simply. "No preconceptions, no local politics influencing our perspective. Plus, you have good instincts for these things."

Mallory smiled at the compliment. Tucker wasn't generous with praise, which made his rare acknowledgments all the more meaningful.

"I've been thinking about the location," she said, grabbing her tablet and bringing up the map. "The body was found on a farm property outside town. Owned by someone named Carl Parsons, according to Gary's notes."

"Farmer's field, middle of nowhere, execution-style killing," Tucker mused. "Suggests the killer's confident, experienced."

"But who hires hits on contractors in small Tennessee towns?" Mallory questioned. "Terry Fisher wasn't wealthy, wasn't involved in drugs, at least not according to the tox screen. He was just a regular guy planning his wedding."

"That's what we're here to find out," Tucker replied.

They lapsed into silence as Duckwood appeared on the horizon. It was a picturesque small town nestled in the rolling hills of eastern Tennessee—red brick buildings lining a traditional Main Street, church steeples rising above the tree line, American flags fluttering from lampposts. It was the kind of place that appeared on postcards captioned "Small Town America."

"Doesn't exactly scream murder capital of Tennessee," Mallory observed as they drove past the Cumberland County Justice Center on the left.

Tucker checked his watch. "Appearances can be deceiving,"

Tucker replied. "It's only ten after ten. We've made good time. Let's drive around a bit, then get some breakfast."

Tucker navigated the quiet streets methodically, giving Mallory a chance to observe the town waking up. Shopkeepers unlocked doors, elderly men gathered at a diner, mothers dropped children at a daycare center. Everything seemed perfectly normal—which made the eleven-year-old unsolved murder seem even more incongruous.

Mallory made mental notes of each location, creating a mental map of the small community. They continued driving, eventually reaching the outskirts where houses gave way to more rural properties.

"That place looks interesting," Tucker said, nodding to the Crossroads Café. "Looks busy. Might be a good place for break-fast and maybe some local gossip. But before we do, I want to take a quick look at the place where the body was found. It should be just... this way," he said as he turned onto a county road that wound through the farmland.

Using GPS coordinates from the case file, they were able to locate the spot where Terry Fisher's body had been discovered eleven years earlier. Now it was just an unremarkable field, part of a working farm with no sign of the tragedy that had occurred there.

"Middle of nowhere," Mallory observed, staring up at the old oak tree, then turning to scan the open landscape. "But close enough to that access road that whoever did it could get in and out quickly."

Tucker nodded. "Local knowledge. Whoever it was that killed him knew this area well."

After surveying the location, they returned to town and stopped at the Crossroads Cafe, a quaint establishment with gingham curtains and the smell of fresh-baked biscuits wafting through the door. A bell jingled as they entered, and several patrons glanced up to assess the newcomers.

They found an empty booth by the window and sat down opposite one another.

A middle-aged waitress approached with a coffeepot in hand. "Hello. I'm Donna," she said as she filled their cups without asking, then set the coffeepot down on the table and pulled a pad from her apron pocket. "Passing through?" she asked conversationally. "What can I get you?"

"We're here on business for a few days," Tucker replied, his voice taking on a slight Southern drawl that Mallory recognized as his "blending in" technique.

"What kind of business brings folks to Duckwood?" Donna asked, her tone friendly but curious.

Tucker kept his answer deliberately vague. "Research. Looking into some local history."

"Well, our breakfast special will keep you fueled for your research," Donna smiled. "All you can eat biscuits and gravy today."

They placed their orders, and Mallory waited until the waitress moved away before leaning across the table. "You didn't mention we're investigating a murder."

"No point raising red flags yet," Tucker replied quietly. "Small towns have efficient gossip networks. By lunchtime, everyone would know why we're here."

Their food arrived quickly; fluffy biscuits smothered in sausage gravy for Tucker, a vegetable omelet for Mallory. They ate quietly, occasionally glancing around the cafe to observe the other patrons.

"So what's our first move after meeting with Gary?" Mallory asked, keeping her voice low.

"Depends on what new information he provides, if any," Tucker replied. "But I do want to speak with Tiffany Springer,

Terry's former fiancée, who married his cousin. That's an unusual development."

"And the police," Mallory added. "We should ask to see and review the full case files if possible."

Tucker nodded. "I'll request a meeting with chief Winson."

After finishing breakfast, they still had a little time before their appointment with Gary. They decided to drive by the Baptist church again, where, according to Gary Fisher's case materials, Terry had been a regular attendee.

The Whitehaven Baptist Church was a white clapboard building with a modest steeple, set back from the road on a well-maintained lot. A sign out front announced Sunday services and Wednesday prayer meetings.

"Pastor Henry Pearcy," Mallory read from the sign. "Same pastor as eleven years ago and, according to Gary's notes, he conducted Terry's funeral."

"Add him to our interview list," Tucker said. "Religious leaders often know more about their congregants than anyone else."

As eleven-thirty approached, they headed to Gary Fisher's address in a modest subdivision on the edge of town. Two children were playing catch in the front yard when they arrived—a teenage boy and a younger girl. The boy noticed them and called back toward the house. A moment later, a tall, slim man with dark hair and a prominent nose appeared at the front door and raised his hand in greeting.

"That must be him," Mallory said, gathering her notebook and digital recorder as they parked in the driveway.

They approached the house, and Fisher extended his hand. "Mr. Randall? Ms. Carver? Gary Fisher. Thank you for coming."

"Call me Tucker, please," Tucker replied, shaking his hand firmly. "And this is Mallory."

"Gary," he responded and offered Mallory his hand. "Please, come inside. My wife Linda has coffee ready."

The modest home was neat and comfortable with family photos prominently displayed. Several showed Terry Fisher—at high school graduation, fishing with an older man who must have been his father, arm-in-arm with a blonde woman Mallory assumed was his fiancée, Tiffany.

Gary led them into a living room where a woman was arranging coffee mugs on a side table. "This is my wife, Linda," he introduced them. "Linda, these are the private investigators I told you about."

Linda nodded politely, but Mallory detected a certain reservation in her manner. Not exactly unwelcoming, but perhaps not entirely comfortable with their presence.

"Thank you for looking into Terry's case," Linda said as they took seats. "It means a lot to Gary, especially with Bill and Margaret's health declining so rapidly."

"How are your parents doing?" Tucker asked Gary directly.

Gary's expression tightened. "Dad's been given two months, maybe three. Lung cancer. Mom's health isn't much better— heart problems. They've held on this long hoping for answers about Terry, but I'm afraid time is running out."

Mallory felt a pang of empathy. She understood all too well the desperate need for closure when a loved one was killed. Her sister Jen had been the same way after Julie's murder—unable to move forward without knowing why her daughter had died.

"We've reviewed the materials you sent," Tucker began, "but we'd like to hear from you directly. Tell us about Terry, what happened, anything you think might help us understand this case better."

Gary took a deep breath, as if mentally preparing himself. "Terry was seven years older than me. We weren't especially close growing up. The age gap made that hard. By the time I was in high school, he was already working as a contractor."

He paused, glancing at a photo of his brother. "About three years before he was killed, when Terry was twenty-five, he started showing some strange habits. Staying out late, being secretive about where he'd been, getting phone calls that he'd take in another room. My parents were worried he might be involved with drugs, but whenever he had drug tests for work, they always came back clean."

"What kind of contracting work did he do?" Mallory asked, jotting notes.

"Home renovations mostly. He was good with his hands, could fix just about anything. He had a solid reputation in town." Gary's pride in his brother was evident in the way he looked at the photograph. "He had his own business. It was small but growing. He was saving to build a house for himself and Tiffany after they got married."

"Tell us about Tiffany," Tucker said. "Your notes mentioned she's now married to your cousin?"

A flicker of discomfort crossed Gary's face. "Yes, to Louis. They got together a few months after Terry died. It was... unexpected. Tiffany took Terry's death hard, completely fell apart at first. Louis helped her through it, and I guess one thing led to another." His tone suggested he had more thoughts on the matter than he was expressing.

"Where does Tiffany live now?" Mallory asked.

"Just a street over, actually. She and Louis have two kids now." Gary hesitated. "She doesn't like talking about Terry anymore. Says it's too painful, and she's moved on. I'm not sure how cooperative she'll be if you try to interview her."

Mallory made a note to visit Tiffany, regardless. Sometimes people who claimed to have moved on were actually holding secrets they were afraid would be discovered if they reopened old wounds.

"Let's talk about the night Terry disappeared," Tucker suggested, steering the conversation back to the central events.

Gary nodded, his expression growing more somber. "It was a Tuesday. Terry had been acting strange for days, according to Tiffany. Distracted, checking his phone a lot. That night, he told her he had to meet someone on business. Didn't say who or what it was about. Just that he'd be back in a couple of hours. That was the last time anyone saw him alive."

"When was his body discovered?" Tucker asked, though they knew the answer from the reports.

"The next morning. A high school kid cutting across Parsons' farm found him." Gary's voice tightened. "Shot twice in the back of the head, left there like garbage. Whoever did it made no attempt to hide the body."

"You mentioned in your notes that the local police investigation seemed inadequate," Mallory prompted. "Can you elaborate on that?"

Gary's expression darkened. "Detective Bradley was in charge initially. He seemed earnest enough, but after a few weeks, the case just... faded away. No arrests, no suspects named publicly, no actual progress."

"What's your opinion of Chief Winson?" Tucker asked carefully.

"Nate?" Gary looked surprised. "He's a good man. Been chief for about six years now. He was just an officer when Terry was killed, so he wasn't in charge of the investigation."

Mallory noted the discrepancy between Gary's positive view of Winson and the online forum posts suggesting corruption. Either Gary was unaware of the rumors, or he didn't believe them.

"We noticed in our research that Pastor Henry Pearcy

conducted Terry's funeral," Mallory observed. "Did Terry attend his church regularly?"

Gary nodded. "Every Sunday. Pastor Henry was a huge support to our family after Terry died. Still is. He visits my parents weekly, even though they're too ill to attend services now."

As they continued talking, Mallory sensed there was something Gary wasn't telling them—some detail or suspicion he was holding back. His answers were forthcoming but occasionally seemed rehearsed, as if he had decided in advance what narrative to present.

Tucker evidently noticed it too, because he shifted tactics, asking more unexpected questions about Terry's friends, his business competitors, any arguments or conflicts he might have had in the weeks before his death.

"Terry got along with everyone," Gary insisted. "That's what made his murder so shocking. He didn't have any enemies."

"Everyone has someone who dislikes them," Mallory pointed out gently. "Even minor disagreements could be relevant."

Gary hesitated, then conceded. "Well, there was some tension with a competitor—Walsh Construction. The owner, Bill Walsh, accused Terry of underbidding him on purpose for a big renovation contract at the high school. But that was just business rivalry, not something worth killing over."

"We'd like to follow up with some of the people you've mentioned," Tucker said as they wrapped up the interview. "Tiffany, Pastor Pearcy, maybe some of Terry's former clients or coworkers. Would you feel comfortable providing their contact information?"

"Of course," Gary agreed quickly. "Anything that might help." He went to his home office and returned with a printed list. "I anticipated you might ask. These are the people who knew Terry best, with their addresses and phone numbers where I have them."

As they stood to leave, Gary suddenly looked hesitant. "There's something else you should know," he said, his voice lower. "Something I didn't put in the emails."

Mallory and Tucker exchanged glances.

"What is it?" Tucker asked.

Gary glanced toward the front yard where his children were still playing, then back to them. "There are rumors in town... about why these men were killed. You know there were more, right? Four more!"

Tucker nodded.

"Rumors about what they might have been involved in."

"We're listening," Mallory encouraged when he paused.

"Some people say there's a... a gunrunning operation. That they move illegal firearms through this area, using the back roads, small private airstrips on farms, that kind of thing." Gary's voice had dropped to nearly a whisper. "I don't know if it's true, but the rumor is that Terry and the others somehow got caught up in it."

"And you didn't include this in your written materials because...?" Tucker prompted.

"Noooo..." he drew the word out. "Because it's just gossip," he said, looking uncomfortable. "And because if it is true, it might be dangerous to put it in writing. These people—if they exist— have been operating for years without getting caught. They've killed before. They wouldn't hesitate to kill again if they felt threatened... would they?"

"As you say," Tucker replied, "it's probably just rumors. We'll look into it, though. In the meantime, say nothing about why we're here. If what you say is true, we do not want to stir the hornet's nest, not yet."

"I won't," Fisher replied. "I'll not say a word. You go careful now."

The warning hung in the air as they said their goodbyes. As they walked back to the SUV, Mallory processed this new information. If Terry Fisher had indeed been involved in gunrunning, it provided both a motive for his murder and an explanation for why the case had never been properly solved. Rural gun smuggling operations often involved local power players; sometimes even law enforcement.

"What do you think?" she asked Tucker as they pulled away from Gary's house.

Tucker's expression was thoughtful. "I think we need to talk to Tiffany Springer; or Tiffany Fisher, as she is now, I suppose. She was the last person to see Terry alive. And I'm increasingly interested in meeting Pastor Pearcy, given his connection to the family."

Mallory nodded. They had their first real lead, their first glimpse beneath the surface of Duckwood's peaceful exterior.

"Where to first?" she asked, already knowing the answer.

"Tiffany's," Tucker confirmed. "Let's see what Terry's fiancée has to say about the man she supposedly loved and the cousin she married after his death."

As they drove through the quiet streets of Duckwood, Mallory couldn't shake the feeling that they were being watched. In a town this small, with secrets this big, strangers asking questions rarely went unnoticed for long. And if Gary's rumors about gunrunning were true, they might already have attracted the attention of some very dangerous people.

The thought should have frightened her, but instead, it only intensified her determination to uncover the truth. Someone had evaded justice for eleven years. Five families had been denied closure. Whatever secrets Duckwood was hiding,

Mallory was resolved to bring them into the light—no matter the risk.

Her phone buzzed with a text from Jen: "Don't forget. Bridal Elegance appt Friday 2pm!!"

Mallory sighed and slipped the phone back into her pocket without responding. Some things would have to wait. Right now, they had a murder to solve.

5

TUCKER PULLED UP TO THE CURB ACROSS THE STREET FROM Tiffany Fisher's address, a two-story home with beige siding and dark green shutters. Like Gary's house, it was in a modest subdivision—newer homes built for middle-class families, each with similar layouts but with different cosmetic details to provide the illusion of uniqueness. A basketball hoop stood in the driveway next to a silver SUV, and carefully tended flower beds lined the front walkway.

"Doesn't exactly scream widow of murder victim, does it?" Mallory remarked, studying the property.

"Very few things are what they appear to be," Tucker replied, turning off the engine. "Especially in cases like this."

He observed the house for a moment longer, noting the children's bicycle leaning against the porch and the American flag hanging beside the front door; outward signs of a normal, stable household. But his years in law enforcement had taught him that the most disturbing crimes often happened behind the most ordinary facades.

"Let's be careful with our questions," he said as they exited the SUV. "If Terry was involved in something illegal, and if

Tiffany knows about it, she might be protective, either out of loyalty to his memory or fear for her own safety."

Mallory nodded. "And if she doesn't know, we don't want to be the ones to shatter her image of him."

They approached the house together, Tucker slightly in the lead. He was aware of Mallory's tendency to dive straight in with the difficult questions, which sometimes yielded surprising confessions but other times shut down interviews before they'd gathered useful information. This situation called for a more measured approach.

Tucker rang the doorbell, and they waited. After about thirty seconds, the door opened to reveal a blonde woman in her early thirties. She was attractive in a carefully maintained way: high-lighted hair styled in a neat bob, subtle makeup, a pastel blouse and khaki capris that suggested she'd dressed for the day but wasn't expecting company.

Her eyes widened slightly as she took in the two strangers on her doorstep. "Can I help you?" she asked.

"Mrs. Fisher?" Tucker asked politely. "I'm Tucker Randall and this is my colleague, Mallory Carver. We're private investigators working with Gary Fisher regarding his brother Terry's case. We were hoping to speak with you for a few minutes, if you have time."

Tiffany's expression flickered through several emotions in rapid succession: surprise, wariness, and something that might have been fear before settling into a carefully neutral look.

"Gary didn't mention he was hiring investigators," she said, her voice was controlled but slightly tight.

"It was a recent decision," Mallory explained. "As you probably know, his parents' health is declining, and he's hoping to bring them some closure."

Tiffany hesitated, glancing past them toward the street as if checking whether any neighbors were watching. Finally, she stepped back. "You might as well come in, I suppose," she said, reluctantly. "I don't have a lot of time, though. I need to pick up my daughter from soccer practice in an hour."

She led them into a living room decorated in the contemporary farmhouse style that had dominated home design shows for the past several years: lots of neutral tones, shiplap accents, and inspirational phrases stenciled on wooden signs. Family photos adorned the walls and side tables, showing Tiffany with a man Tucker assumed was Louis Fisher and two children—a boy around eleven and a girl about nine.

"Please, sit down," Tiffany waved a hand toward a beige sectional sofa. "Can I get you anything? Water? Coffee?"

"We're fine, thank you," Tucker replied, taking a seat while maintaining eye contact. "We appreciate you taking the time to speak with us."

Tiffany settled into an armchair across from them, her posture straight, hands folded in her lap. "What exactly do you want to know? It's been eleven years, and I've told the police everything I know multiple times."

Tucker nodded understandingly. "We're aware of your previous statements, but sometimes details that seemed insignificant at the time become important with new perspectives. We're hoping you might help us understand Terry better; who he was, what was happening in his life in the weeks before his death."

It was a deliberate strategy to start broadly rather than zeroing in on the night of Terry's disappeared. Tucker wanted to establish rapport, get Tiffany talking comfortably before addressing more sensitive areas.

"Terry was..." Tiffany paused, seeming to search for the right words. "He was charming. Hardworking. Everyone liked him." Her description was positive but generic, the kind of bland eulogy that revealed little of substance.

"How did you two meet?" Mallory asked, her tone conversational.

A genuine smile flickered across Tiffany's face for the first time. "High school. He was a senior when I was a sophomore. We didn't start dating until after he graduated, though. My parents wouldn't have allowed it otherwise."

"And you were engaged to be married when he died?" Tucker prompted.

Tiffany nodded, twisting a ring on her right hand, not her wedding band, but perhaps a memento from her relationship with Terry. "We'd been engaged for almost a year. The wedding was scheduled for that June."

"That must have been devastating," Mallory whispered.

"It was." Tiffany's voice tightened. "I didn't think I'd ever recover. Louis—my husband now—he really helped me through that time. He was Terry's cousin, so he was grieving, too. We understood each other's pain."

Tucker watched her carefully as she spoke. There was genuine emotion there, but also what appeared to be rehearsed elements, as if she'd told this version of events many times and had settled on a narrative that was both true and carefully curated.

"Gary mentioned that in the weeks before Terry died, he'd been acting differently," Tucker said. "Staying out late, being secretive about phone calls. Did you notice these changes as well?"

Tiffany's posture stiffened slightly. "Yes. He said it was work-related—a big project he was bidding on. I didn't question it much. Terry was ambitious, always looking for ways to grow his business."

"But you were concerned enough to mention it to the police after his death," Tucker noted, referencing her initial statement from the case file.

Her eyes narrowed slightly. "Only because they asked if I'd noticed anything unusual. In hindsight, maybe I should have paid more attention, asked more questions. But you can't change the past, can you?"

The defensiveness in her tone was subtle, but unmistakable. Tucker changed tack, moving to a seemingly unrelated topic. "Terry was religious, I understand? A regular at Pastor Pearcy's church?"

The question seemed to catch Tiffany off guard. "Yes. We both were. Pastor Henry was very supportive after... after what happened."

"He conducted the funeral service?" Tucker asked.

"Yes. It was beautiful, actually. He talked about Terry's spirit, his good heart." Tiffany's expression softened momentarily. "Pastor Henry has a way of bringing comfort even in the darkest times."

Tucker nodded sympathetically. "And the night Terry disappeared; you were the last person to see him, correct?"

The shift back to the central event was deliberate, coming after Tiffany had relaxed slightly while discussing the pastor. Her guard went up again immediately.

"As far as I know, yes. He left our apartment around nine. Said he had to meet someone about work, though it seemed late for a business meeting."

"Did he say who he was meeting?" Mallory asked.

"No. Just that it wouldn't take long and not to wait up." Tiffany looked down at her hands. "I fell asleep watching TV. When I woke up around two in the morning and he wasn't home, I tried calling his cell phone. It went straight to voicemail."

"What did you do then?" Tucker prompted.

"Nothing, at first. It wasn't completely out of character for Terry to work late. I figured he'd gotten caught up in something and would be home soon." Her voice caught slightly. "By morning, when he still wasn't back and wasn't answering calls, I called his parents, then Gary. We were about to file a missing person report when..."

She trailed off, and Tucker finished the thought for her. "When Terry's body was found on the Parsons' property."

Tiffany nodded, blinking rapidly. "It was surreal," she said. "Like a nightmare I couldn't wake up from. One minute we're planning our wedding, the next I'm planning his funeral."

Tucker allowed a moment of respectful silence before continuing. "Tiffany, in the years since, have you heard any theories about why Terry was killed?"

She hesitated, glancing toward a window. "What do you mean?"

"Small town talk," Mallory interjected gently. "Especially about unsolved murders. There must have been rumors, speculations about what Terry might have been involved in."

Tiffany's gaze snapped to Mallory. "Involved in? Terry wasn't 'involved' in anything. He was a good man who was in the wrong place at the wrong time."

The defensiveness was revealing. Tucker pressed further, keeping his tone casual. "Of course. But Gary mentioned there are rumors around town about gunrunning, illegal activities that might have led to these murders. Five men killed the same way over eleven years. That suggests something serious."

Tiffany stood abruptly. "I don't know anything about that. And I don't appreciate you coming into my home and suggesting Terry was mixed up in something criminal. He wasn't that kind of person."

Tucker remained seated, maintaining a calm demeanor despite her agitation. "We're not suggesting anything, Mrs. Fisher. We're just trying to understand all the possibilities.

Terry's parents deserve to know what happened to their son before they pass."

"And you think I don't want that?" Tiffany's voice rose slightly. "Terry was the love of my life. His death destroyed me. But dragging his name through the mud won't bring him back or give anyone closure."

Mallory adopted a softer approach. "We understand this is difficult, Tiffany," she said, softly. "But sometimes people get caught up in situations without fully understanding what they're involved in. If Terry was in trouble, or if he witnessed something he shouldn't have, that information could help us find who killed him."

Tiffany seemed to struggle with herself for a moment before her shoulders sagged. "Look, I don't know anything concrete. But..." she lowered her voice, glancing toward the hallway as if ensuring no one else was listening, "about a week before he died, I found a gun in his truck. A handgun. Terry never owned firearms. He didn't even like them. When I asked him about it, he got defensive, said it was for protection, that times were changing."

Tucker leaned forward slightly. "Did he elaborate on what he needed protection from?"

"No. And I didn't push it. We had a big fight about the wedding venue that same day, so the gun conversation got lost in that." She twisted her hands together. "I've always wondered if I should have asked more questions, if I could have somehow prevented what happened."

"You couldn't have known," Mallory assured her. "Did you tell the police about the gun?"

Tiffany nodded. "I told Detective Bradley. He made a note of it, but I don't think anything ever came of it. The gun wasn't on Terry when they found him."

This was new information, something not mentioned in the

police reports Gary had provided. Either it had been deliberately omitted, or the paperwork had been lost over the years.

"When did you start dating Louis?" Tucker asked, the question seemingly coming out of nowhere.

Tiffany blinked at the abrupt change of subject. "What does that have to do with anything?"

"I'm just trying to establish a timeline," Tucker replied calmly.

She exhaled slowly. "I don't... About four months after Terry died. Louis had been checking on me regularly; bringing groceries, helping with household repairs, things like that. It evolved..." She paused, twisting her fingers together. "It evolved naturally," she continued. "We were both grieving. We understood each other."

"And Terry's family; were they supportive of the relationship?" Tucker asked.

A flash of something—guilt, perhaps, or maybe defiance—crossed Tiffany's face. "Not initially. Gary especially thought it was too soon, disrespectful to Terry's memory. His parents were more understanding. They've always liked Louis."

Tucker nodded, mentally filing away the information. "Just one more question, Tiffany. Did Terry ever mention anything about the other victims? Cory Robar, Samuel Jenkins, Malik Williams, or Freddy Paul?"

Tiffany frowned. "I recognize Cory's name—he did some work for the school district—but I don't think Terry ever mentioned him specifically. I don't know the others at all. Why?"

"They were all killed the same way as Terry over the past eleven years," Mallory explained. "Two shots to the back of the head, bodies left in similar rural locations around Duckwood."

Tiffany's face paled. "I knew about a couple of other murders, but not four. That's... that's horrible."

"Yet the police never publicly connected the cases," Tucker observed, watching her reaction carefully.

"Small towns," Tiffany said with a faint, bitter smile. "Things get buried, don't they? Forgotten. Life goes on. That's the way it is here." She glanced at her watch. "I'm sorry, but I really do need to leave soon to pick up my daughter."

Tucker recognized the dismissal and rose to his feet. "Thank you for your time, Mrs. Fisher. If you think of anything else, no matter how insignificant it might seem, please call us." He handed her a business card.

Tiffany accepted it reluctantly. "I've told you everything I know. And I'd appreciate it if you didn't mention to Louis that we spoke. He... he thinks I should leave the past in the past. He worries about me getting upset."

"Of course," Mallory assured her. "We understand."

6

As THEY WALKED BACK TO THE SUV, TUCKER PROCESSED THE interview, mentally cataloging what had been said and, perhaps more importantly, what had been deliberately avoided. Tiffany had been cooperative on the surface but guarded in substance. The revelation about the gun was significant, but Tucker suspected there was more she wasn't sharing.

Once they were inside the vehicle, Mallory took her recorder from her jacket pocket, turned to him expectantly, wagged it in the air and said, "Well? What do you think?"

"I think she's hiding something," Tucker replied, starting the engine. "The question is whether it's something directly related to Terry's murder, or just uncomfortable details about their relationship that she'd rather keep private."

"The gun is interesting," Mallory noted. "If Terry wasn't typically a gun owner, why suddenly have one for 'protection' a week before his death? He must have felt threatened."

Tucker nodded. "And it wasn't found with his body, which suggests either the killer took it, or Terry hid it somewhere before the meeting that led to his death."

"What about her relationship with Louis? Starting to date

your murdered fiancé's cousin within a few months seems... fast."

"People process grief differently," Tucker said, not entirely dismissing the observation. "But it's worth looking into Louis Fisher more thoroughly. If Terry was involved in something illegal, Louis might have known about it. They were cousins, after all."

They drove in silence for a few moments, each considering the implications of Tiffany's statements and body language. Duckwood passed by outside the windows, its quiet streets and modest businesses concealing what was clearly a more complex and dangerous reality than first appearances suggested.

"Where to next?" Mallory asked. "Pastor Pearcy?"

Tucker checked his watch. "It's nearly lunchtime. Let's grab something to eat and review what we've learned so far. I'd also like to stop by the police station to see if we can speak with Chief Winson, and I'd like to track down Detective Bradley, even if he's retired."

"The pastor conducted all five funeral services," Mallory reminded him. "That can't be coincidence."

"Agreed, but in a town this size, there might only be one or two churches. We'll definitely speak with him, but let's be methodical about it."

They found a small deli near the town square and secured a booth in the corner, where they could talk privately while observing the other patrons. Tucker ordered a turkey sandwich, Mallory a salad, and they spread their notes across the table while they waited.

"So far we have a gun that appeared shortly before Terry's death, rumors of gunrunning in the area, five victims killed in the same manner over eleven years, a fiancée who married the victim's cousin, and a pastor who conducted all the funeral services," Tucker summarized. "Plus a police department that either couldn't or wouldn't connect the cases."

"And Gary's parents dying without answers after more than a decade," Mallory added, her expression softening with empathy. "That's the part that gets me. Imagine living all those years not knowing who killed your child or why."

Tucker nodded, understanding her connection to that aspect of the case. Mallory had seen firsthand how Julie's murder had devastated her sister Jen's family. That personal experience undoubtedly fueled her determination to solve cold cases like Terry Fisher's.

"Let's focus on the gunrunning angle," Tucker suggested. "If Terry suddenly had a gun for protection, it suggests he might have been involved in something dangerous or had knowledge of something dangerous."

"But if he was part of a gunrunning operation, why would he need protection from his own associates?" Mallory questioned. "Unless... Unless he was planning to leave or threaten exposure."

"Exactly. If Terry wanted out, or if he was going to talk to authorities, that would give the organization motive to silence him."

As they continued discussing theories, Tucker noticed a man in uniform enter the deli. He was in his mid-forties, with a solid build and the confident bearing of someone used to authority. Several patrons nodded respectfully as he passed, and the server behind the counter immediately began preparing what appeared to be his usual order without him having to ask.

"I'm guessing that's Chief Winson," Tucker murmured to Mallory, who glanced over her shoulder casually.

"Should we approach him?" she asked.

Tucker considered the options. "Not here. Too public. Let's finish up and head to the station formally. Better to establish ourselves as professionals conducting an investigation rather than ambush him during his lunch break."

They paid their bill and left, Mallory resisting the urge to stare at the police chief as they passed. Once outside, they walked back to their SUV, parked a block away.

"I've been thinking about the gun," Mallory said as they walked. "What if it wasn't for protection? What if Terry was actually delivering it as part of the operation? Or maybe he found it and was concerned about it?"

"All possibilities are worth considering," Tucker agreed. "But without the weapon itself, it's hard to draw conclusions. I'd like to know if it was ever logged in as evidence, or if that detail somehow disappeared from the official record."

As they approached their vehicle, Tucker spotted something tucked under the windshield wiper. He glanced around, checking to see if anyone was watching them, but the street was busy with normal lunchtime activity. No one was paying them particular attention.

"What's that?" Mallory asked as he carefully removed what appeared to be a folded piece of paper.

Tucker unfolded it, a handwritten note that read: "Stop asking questions about Terry Fisher. Leave Duckwood while you can. This is your only warning."

He handed it to Mallory, who read it quickly, her eyes widening. "Well," she said with a grim smile, "looks like we're on the right track. Someone's nervous."

"Or someone's trying to protect us," Tucker countered, examining the paper for any identifying marks or characteristics. The handwriting was deliberately disguised, printed in all capital letters with no distinctive flourishes.

"You think it's a genuine warning rather than a threat?" Mallory asked.

"Could be either," Tucker admitted, carefully placing the

note in an evidence bag from his pocket. "But it confirms what we've suspected; there's something significant connecting these murders, and there are people in Duckwood who know more than they're saying."

As he scanned the surrounding buildings and parked cars, his law enforcement instincts on high alert, Tucker made a decision. "Let's head to the police station now. We'll report this, establish an official record of our presence and purpose in Duckwood."

"And watch how Chief Winson reacts," Mallory added, catching onto his strategy.

"Exactly." Tucker opened the car door for her before walking around to the driver's side. "But we'll keep certain details to ourselves for now; particularly our suspicions about gunrunning and potential police involvement. You have your weapon with you, I assume."

"Always," she replied.

As they drove the short distance to the Duckwood Police Department, Tucker couldn't shake the feeling that they'd stirred up something dangerous, something that had remained hidden for eleven years and wouldn't easily be exposed. The threatening note was a tangible reminder that their investigation carried real risks.

Whatever secrets Duckwood was hiding, powerful people wanted them to remain buried. But Tucker hadn't resigned from the FBI to let injustice prevail elsewhere. Five men had been murdered, five families had been left without answers. He and Mallory would get to the truth, no matter the cost.

7

MALLORY FOLLOWED TUCKER THROUGH THE GLASS DOORS INTO the Duckwood Police Department, between Highland Avenue and Archer Street, next to Duckwood Fire and Rescue. They entered the reception area and stepped up to the desk behind which sat a middle-aged female officer. A bulletin board on the wall displayed community notices and wanted posters, while a glass case nearby housed trophies from police softball tournaments and community service awards.

Small-town law enforcement at its most stereotypical, she thought, approaching the reception desk beside Tucker.

"Can I help you?" The receptionist glanced up from her computer, her expression professionally neutral but her eyes curious.

Tucker produced his identification. "Tucker Randall and Mallory Carver. We're private investigators from Chattanooga working on behalf of the Fisher family regarding the Terry Fisher case. We'd like to speak with Chief Winson, if he's available."

The woman's eyebrows rose slightly. "The Fisher case? That's going back some years." She picked up her phone. "Let me see if the chief is available."

While she made the call, Mallory studied the room more carefully. A framed photo on the wall showed the current police force—forty sworn officers, including the chief, posed in three lines, one behind the other. Another showed what appeared to be a retirement party, with an older man receiving a plaque while surrounded by colleagues. The name plate read "Detective James Bradley, 35 Years of Service."

"Chief Winson can see you," the receptionist announced, hanging up the phone. "Last door on the right."

Tucker thanked her, and they walked down the hallway. Mallory noted the building's layout, a habit she'd developed over her three years of investigative work. Two interview rooms, a break room, a half dozen offices, a situation room, a door marked "Evidence," an unmarked door at the end of the corridor and, finally, the chief's office on the right.

The door was open when they reached it. Chief Nate Winson was seated behind a desk cluttered with paperwork, a half-eaten sandwich from the deli they'd just left pushed to one side. He was better looking up close than Mallory had observed from across the deli—early forties, athletic build, salt-and-pepper hair cut in a military style, and sharp green eyes that assessed them with professional interest.

"Come in," he said, gesturing to two chairs opposite his desk. "I understand you're looking into the Fisher case. That's ancient history around here."

"Not for Gary Fisher and his parents," Mallory replied before she could stop herself. Tucker gave her a subtle glance, a reminder of their agreement that he would lead this conversation.

Winson's expression didn't change. "Of course not. That poor family never got closure. Please, sit down."

They settled into the chairs, and Tucker smoothly took control of the conversation. "Thank you for seeing us, Chief. We've been retained by Gary Fisher to review his brother's case, considering his parents' declining health."

"Understandable," Winson nodded. "Though I'm not sure what you expect to find after eleven years that our department and the sheriff's office couldn't."

"Fresh eyes sometimes help," Tucker said diplomatically. "And we're hoping you might provide access to the original case files. The copies we have are incomplete."

Winson leaned back in his chair, studying them. "I wasn't chief when Terry Fisher was killed. Wasn't even the lead detective. That was Jim Bradley. He's retired now. I was just a patrol officer."

"But you're familiar with the case?" Mallory asked.

"Everyone in the department is familiar with it," Winson replied. "Unsolved murders aren't common around here, thankfully. And the Fisher family has been... persistent in keeping it on our radar."

There was something in his tone when he said "persistent" that caught Mallory's attention—not quite resentment, but a subtle sign that the family's efforts were viewed as an irritation rather than a rightful pursuit of justice.

"We've also become aware of four similar murders in the area over the past eleven years," Tucker said, watching the chief carefully. "Cory Robar, Samuel Jenkins, Malik Williams, and Freddy Paul. All killed in the same manner as Terry Fisher, all found within a five-mile radius."

Chief Winson's expression tightened almost imperceptibly. "Those cases aren't officially connected."

"But unofficially?" Mallory pressed.

The chief sighed. "Look, I understand what you're doing. You're trying to build a narrative, connect dots to give the family answers. But sometimes coincidences are just coincidences."

"Five execution-style murders in a small rural community within eleven years doesn't strike me as coincidental," Tucker observed calmly.

"When you've been in law enforcement as long as I have, you learn that pattern recognition can be misleading," Winson countered. "Yes, the MO is similar. But these men had different backgrounds, different social circles. We've never found a concrete connection between them."

Mallory bit back a skeptical response, letting Tucker continue the conversation. She focused instead on observing the chief, his body language, his eye contact, the subtle tells that might show he was being less than forthcoming.

"We'd still appreciate access to the files," Tucker said. "For all five cases, if possible. It would help us be thorough in our report to the Fisher family."

Winson hesitated, then nodded. "I can arrange that. But I'll need to have someone from the department present while you review them. Chain of custody, you understand?"

"Of course," Tucker agreed. "There's another matter we'd like to discuss as well." He reached into his pocket and produced the threatening note they'd found on their SUV. "This was left on our vehicle while we were having lunch."

Winson took the evidence bag, examining the note with a frown. "How long have you been in town?"

"Since this morning," Mallory answered. "We interviewed Gary Fisher and Tiffany Fisher, drove by the locations where the bodies were discovered, and had lunch at the deli."

"And someone's already warning you off," Winson mused, setting the note on his desk. "Interesting."

"We thought you should be aware," Tucker said. "In case there are other incidents."

The chief nodded. "I appreciate that. I'll have one of my officers take your statement and file a report." He seemed to consider something before continuing. "I should warn you—Duckwood is a close-knit community. People here don't appreciate outsiders stirring up old troubles."

"We're not here to cause trouble," Mallory assured him. "We just want the truth."

"The truth," Winson repeated, with a slight smile that didn't reach his eyes. "In my experience, that's rarely as straightforward as people hope." He stood up, signaling the end of the meeting. "I'll have Officer Daniels supervise your review of the case files tomorrow morning, if that works for you. And I'll assign someone to take your statement about this note."

"We'd also like to speak with Detective Bradley," Tucker added, remaining seated. "I understand he's retired now, but as the original investigator, he might have insights that aren't in the official reports."

Something flickered across Winson's face; reluctance, perhaps, or concern. "Jim's in the Golden Years Retirement Home on the edge of town. His health isn't great, and his memory comes and goes. I can't guarantee he'll be helpful."

"We'd still like to try," Mallory said.

"Your prerogative," Winson shrugged. "Just don't get your hopes up. And don't upset him. The staff there is protective."

As if on cue, a knock came at the office door, and a young officer appeared. "Sorry to interrupt, Chief, but the mayor's on line one. Says it's urgent."

Winson nodded. "I need to take this," he said. "Officer Daniels will help you with your statement about the threat." He extended his hand to Tucker, then Mallory. "Good luck with your investigation. I hope you find what you're looking for."

Mallory couldn't help but notice he didn't say he hoped they solved the case.

Officer Daniels, a fresh-faced young man who couldn't have been more than twenty-five, led them to an interview room where he took their statement about the threatening note. He seemed earnest and thorough, asking detailed questions about the exact location of their vehicle, whether they had noticed anyone suspicious, and if they had received any other threats.

"Does this sort of thing happen often in Duckwood?" Mallory asked casually while Daniels was writing.

He looked up, surprised. "No, ma'am. We're a peaceful town, generally speaking. Some drunk and disorderlies on weekends, occasional domestic disputes, teenagers causing mischief, but threatening notes? That's unusual."

"What about the murders we're investigating?" Tucker inquired. "Those aren't exactly 'peaceful town' activities."

Daniels shifted uncomfortably. "That's different. Those were... isolated incidents. And they happened over many years." He cleared his throat. "Have you folks arranged accommodation while you're in town?"

The change of subject wasn't subtle, but Mallory went with it. "We're staying at the Duckwood Inn. Why?"

"Just asking," Daniels said, looking back down at his form. "In case we need to reach you." He completed the report and slid it across the table for them to sign.

After finishing with Officer Daniels, they left the station and returned to their vehicle. Mallory waited until they were inside, with the doors closed, before speaking.

"Well, that was enlightening," she said, her voice low despite being alone. "Winson is definitely holding back."

Tucker nodded as he started the engine. "The question is whether it's because he's involved, or because he genuinely doesn't believe the cases are connected."

"Did you notice how quickly he changed the subject when

you mentioned Detective Bradley? Almost like he didn't want us talking to him."

"I caught that," Tucker agreed. "Which means Bradley moves to the top of our priority list. Let's head to the Golden Years now and see if he's in any condition to speak with us."

8

THE GOLDEN YEARS RETIREMENT HOME WAS A SINGLE-STORY brick building on the outskirts of town surrounded by several acres of well-maintained gardens. A covered porch with rocking chairs fronted the entrance, though no residents were outside in the afternoon heat.

Inside, the facility was clean and bright, with a faint smell of industrial cleaner barely masking the underlying scent of age and illness. A cheerful woman at the reception desk greeted them with a practiced smile.

"We're here to see James Bradley," Tucker explained.

"Are you relatives?" she asked, frowning.

"No, ma'am," Tucker replied. "We're private investigators working on a case he handled years ago."

The woman's smile faltered slightly. "Well..." She hesitated, then continued, "Mr. Bradley doesn't get many visitors except for his daughter. And his condition..." Again, she hesitated.

"We understand he has memory issues," Mallory said gently. "But we'd like to try. It's for the family of a murder victim."

The appeal to empathy worked. The receptionist nodded.

"Let me check to see if he's having a good day. Sometimes mornings are better than afternoons for him."

She made a quick call, then directed them to a sunroom at the back of the facility. "Twenty minutes, please. Don't tire him out."

They found Bradley sitting in a wheelchair by a large window overlooking a garden, a blanket draped over his legs despite the warm day. He was thin, his once-powerful frame now diminished with age, his white hair neatly combed to one side, and his eyes, though clouded with cataracts, still held a sharp intelligence.

"Detective Bradley?" Tucker approached, extending his hand. "I'm Tucker Randall, and this is my colleague, Mallory Carver. We're private investigators looking into the Terry Fisher case."

Bradley's hand was cool and papery as he shook Tucker's, then Mallory's. "Fisher," he repeated, his voice stronger than his appearance suggested. "Terry Fisher. He was found on Pearcy's land."

Mallory glanced at Tucker. This didn't sound like someone with severe memory issues. They sat in chairs opposite Bradley, positioning themselves where he could see them clearly.

"That's right," Mallory confirmed. "You were the detective in charge of the investigation."

Bradley nodded slowly. "Shot twice in the back of the head. Execution-style. No casings found. Professional job."

"Do you remember anything specific about the case that might not have made it into the official reports?" Tucker asked.

The old detective was quiet for a moment, his gaze drifting to the garden outside. "You know about the others?" he finally asked.

"Cory Robar, Samuel Jenkins, Malik Williams, and Freddy

Paul," Mallory listed. "All killed the same way over the past decade."

"All within five miles of each other. All just inside the city limits," Bradley added. "I always thought that was significant. We started calling it 'the Graveyard,' you know. Just among ourselves. Not officially, of course. Officially, they were separate cases."

"Why?" Tucker pressed gently. "Why not investigate them as connected homicides?"

Bradley's eyes shifted back to them, suddenly sharper. "Politics. Money. The usual reasons. Duckwood depends on tourism from the lake, the golf, the state park, and so on, and on being seen as a safe, quiet community. Serial killings are bad for business."

"So you were told to keep the cases separate?" Mallory asked, leaning forward.

"Not in so many words," Bradley replied. "But the message was clear. Especially after I started asking questions about certain local businesses, certain shipments coming through the area."

Tucker and Mallory exchanged glances. "What kind of shipments?" Tucker asked.

Bradley's gaze drifted again, and for a moment, Mallory worried they'd lost him. Then he focused on them with renewed clarity. "Guns. Modified automatic weapons. Coming up from the south, passing through here on the way north and east. Using the back roads, the lake access points. Terry Fisher... I always thought he must have been involved, or that maybe he witnessed something he shouldn't. Either way, if he talked to the wrong person..." He trailed off with a slight shrug.

"Do you know who was behind the operation?" Mallory asked, frowning, inwardly excited by this confirmation of their suspicions.

Bradley shook his head slowly. "Never got that far," he replied. "After I started pulling on those threads, I had an accident. Nasty fall down the stairs at home. Three broken ribs, concussion. When I came back to work, the Fisher case was officially cold, and I was assigned to petty theft and vandalism until I retired." His rheumy eyes held a mixture of regret and resignation. "I knew when to take a hint."

"The other victims," Tucker prompted. "Do you think they were connected to the same gunrunning operation?"

"Had to be," Bradley nodded. "Too many similarities otherwise. But I never got to investigate properly. By the time the second victim turned up, I was already sidelined."

"What about Nate Winson?" Mallory asked. "Was he involved in any way?"

Bradley's expression closed off slightly. "Nate was a good officer. Young, ambitious. Didn't ask too many questions, which is how you advance in a department like ours." He paused. "That's all I'll say about the current chief."

A nurse appeared in the doorway. "Mr. Bradley needs his medication and rest now."

Sensing they wouldn't get much more, Tucker handed Bradley a card. "If you remember anything else, or if you're willing to talk again, please call us."

Bradley took the card, studying it before tucking it into the pocket of his cardigan. "Be careful," he said quietly. "Duckwood looks peaceful, but the currents run deep. People who ask the wrong questions tend to have accidents."

"Like falling down stairs?" Mallory asked.

The old detective's eyes met hers. "Among other things," he confirmed.

The nurse wheeled Bradley away, leaving Tucker and Mallory alone in the sunroom. They remained silent for a moment, both aware that conversations in such facilities often carried.

"You get all that?" Tucker asked, referring to her recorder.

She nodded, patted her pocket, and said, "Of course."

"Then let's go," Tucker said, rising to his feet.

9

TWO MINUTES LATER, WITHOUT SAYING ANOTHER WORD TO EACH other, they stepped out into the sunshine.

"Well, that confirms the gunrunning theory," Mallory said once they were safely inside the vehicle. "And it suggests local law enforcement was pressured into keeping the cases separate and unsolved."

"But it doesn't tell us who's behind it," Tucker pointed out. "Or why these men were killed."

"At least we know we're on the right track, though," Mallory replied. "And Bradley seemed much more coherent than Winson would have us to believe."

"Another reason to be skeptical of the chief," Tucker exclaimed as he started the engine. "Let's regroup at the hotel and review what we've learned today and plan our next steps."

The Duckwood Inn was a modest two-story motel with a new red metal roof and located on the edge of town. Its vintage neon sign and recently repainted exterior suggesting an estab-lishment trying to maintain standards despite limited resources. Their room was on the second floor, simple but clean, with two queen beds, a small table with two chairs, and a bathroom with a coffee maker that had been updated sometime in the early 2000s. It was generic, and just like a million other hotel rooms scattered across the United States from east to west and one end to the other.

Tucker dumped his suitcase on the bed nearest the window, leaving the one closest to the bathroom for Mallory, and placed his briefcase on the table. Then he went to the minibar, took out two soft drinks, spread their notes on his bed while Mallory took a seat at the small table and opened her laptop.

"So we have confirmation of gunrunning through Duckwood, five victims killed the same way, a detective whose investigation was deliberately derailed, and a police chief who seems reluctant to acknowledge any connection between the cases," she summarized, typing as she spoke.

"Plus a threatening note warning us to leave town, a fiancée who married the victim's cousin and seems to be hiding something, and a pastor who conducted all five funeral services," Tucker added. "It's starting to take shape, but we're still missing the key connections."

Mallory nodded, scrolling through the notes they'd compiled. "Let's focus on the gun angle," she said. "If Terry had a gun for protection shortly before his death, it suggests he knew he was in danger."

"Or maybe he wasn't part of it at all," Tucker suggested. "Maybe he simply stumbled onto something, acquired the gun for protection, and was killed before he could go to authorities."

"Either way, the gun is significant," Mallory agreed. "And it's not mentioned in the official reports we have, despite Tiffany saying she told Detective Bradley about it."

"Tomorrow, we'll review the complete case files," Tucker said. "See if there's any mention of it there, or if that detail was deliberately removed."

Mallory shifted her focus. "What about this Pastor Pearcy?

Bradley said Terry was found on 'Pearcy's land,' but Gary told us it was the Parsons' farm."

Tucker frowned. "That's a discrepancy worth exploring. Could be Bradley's memory playing tricks, or it could be significant. We should talk to the pastor tomorrow, see what he knows."

"And Louis Fisher," Mallory added. "Tiffany's current husband, Terry's cousin. He might have insights that Tiffany wasn't willing to share."

They continued planning their investigation until the early evening, ordering pizza delivered to their room rather than risk being overheard in a local restaurant. As they ate, Mallory's phone rang. She looked at the screen. It was Jen calling, as promised.

"I should take this," she said, stepping out onto the walkway for privacy.

"Hey," she answered, watching the sun beginning to set over Duckwood.

"Finally!" Jen's voice came through. "I was starting to worry. How's the mysterious cold case going?"

"Interestingly," Mallory replied, careful not to share any details over the phone, "we're making progress."

"Enough progress that you'll be back for the dress appointment on Friday? The boutique had a cancellation, and it's the only slot they have for weeks."

Mallory hesitated. Two days from now? It was possible they'd wrap up the investigation by then, but unlikely given the layers of complexity they were uncovering.

"I'll try, Jen. But this case is important, and complex. It could take a while."

She heard her sister's sigh. "Your wedding is important too, Mal. Six months will go by faster than you think."

"I know, I know," Mallory assured her. "Look, if I can't make it back by Friday, maybe you could FaceTime me from the appointment? I trust your judgment anyway."

They chatted a few minutes longer before ending the call. When Mallory returned inside, Tucker was reviewing a map of the area, marking the locations where each body had been found.

"Everything okay?" he asked, glancing up.

"Just wedding stuff," Mallory replied, sitting beside him on the bed. "Jen's worried I won't make it back for a dress appointment."

Tucker studied her face. "If you need to go back for that, I can handle things here for a day."

The offer was generous, especially given their growing concerns about the case's danger. But Mallory shook her head. "No, we're partners in this. The dress can wait."

Tucker's expression softened slightly. "You're sure?"

"Positive," she affirmed, turning her attention back to the map. "So, what's next for tomorrow?"

"Case files in the morning, then the pastor, if he's available. We should try to track down Louis Fisher as well." Tucker circled the area where the bodies had been found. "And I think we need to physically check out this area again, more thoroughly this time. Bradley called it 'the Graveyard' for a reason. There might be something about the location itself that's significant."

"He mentioned they were all found just inside the city limits," Mallory said, nodding. "Why would he do that? Why would that be significant?" she asked, though she thought she already knew the answer.

Tucker glanced at her, then said, "Whoever killed them may have planned it that way. Outside the city limit the sheriff's office would have had jurisdiction. As it is, it's Chief Winson's purview. Kind of convenient, don't you think?"

Mallory nodded. "That's what I thought," she replied thoughtfully. She was excited despite the long day. They were making progress, piecing together a puzzle that had remained unsolved for over a decade. It was exhilarating, and whatever dangers might lie ahead, the promise of justice for Terry Fisher and the other victims was worth the risk.

As night fell over Duckwood, Mallory couldn't shake the feeling that they were being watched. The threatening note, Bradley's warning about "accidents," the chief's carefully measured responses—all suggested they were stirring up trouble for some powerful people who wanted the past to remain buried.

And the note on the windshield? That made it personal.

10

THEY ARRIVED AT THE DUCKWOOD POLICE DEPARTMENT PRECISELY at eight-thirty the next morning. Tucker had been awake since five, reviewing their notes and planning their approach. Experience had taught him that when examining cold case files, organization and focus were essential. They needed to identify discrepancies, missing information, and connections that previous investigators had either missed or deliberately ignored.

Officer Daniels was waiting for them in the reception area, his demeanor professional but slightly nervous. "Chief Winson asked me to supervise your review of the case files," he explained, leading them down a hallway to a small conference room. "I'll need to remain present while you examine them."

"Understood," Tucker replied, noting the young officer's discomfort. Daniels couldn't be much more than a rookie, probably assigned to this task because the chief wanted someone who wouldn't provide additional insights.

Five cardboard boxes were arranged on the conference table, each labeled with a victim's name. Tucker immediately noticed that Terry Fisher's box was significantly larger than the others.

"The Fisher case received the most thorough investigation,"

Daniels explained, following Tucker's gaze. "It was the first, and Detective Bradley was... very methodical."

Tucker nodded, pulling a pair of latex gloves from his pocket and putting them on before opening the first box. Mallory did the same, settling into a chair across from him. They had agreed to each focus on different aspects—Tucker would examine the forensic evidence and official reports, while Mallory would review witness statements and personal effects.

The first folder contained autopsy photos of Terry Fisher. Despite his years of law enforcement experience, Tucker had never completely desensitized to such images. The young man lay face-down in tall grass, two neat bullet holes visible at the base of his skull. The clinical precision of the wounds confirmed what they already knew: this was no crime of passion. It was a calculated execution.

The medical examiner's report estimated the time of death to be between eleven in the evening and one in the morning on the night Terry disappeared. Cause of death: two gunshot wounds to the occipital region of the skull, fired at close range. The bullets had passed through the brain and exited through the frontal bone. No bullet casings had been found at the scene, suggesting either they were collected by the killer or a revolver was used.

Tucker turned to the ballistics report. One of the bullets had been recovered from a tree trunk at the scene, a 9mm, consistent with numerous handgun models. Without casings or the weapon itself, more specific identification had been impossible.

Next came the crime scene photos and diagrams. Tucker studied them carefully, noting the rural setting, the lack of cover that would have made the shooting visible from a distance, should anyone have been nearby. The body had been found approximately fifty yards from a dirt access road that connected to a county highway.

"Officer Daniels," Tucker said without looking up, "whose property was Terry Fisher's body found on? These reports list it as belonging to Carl Parsons, but Detective Bradley referred to it as Pearcy's land."

The young officer shifted uncomfortably. "I believe it's the Parsons' farm, sir. But Pastor Pearcy leases part of it from Carl Parsons for his church's annual events. Has done for years."

Tucker noted this information, exchanging a glance with Mallory. They hadn't known about this connection.

As he continued through the file, Tucker found statements from the initial responding officers, Detective Bradley's detailed notes from the first forty-eight hours, and canvass reports from nearby properties. All appeared thorough and professionally executed. But when he reached the evidence log, something caught his attention.

"There's no mention here of a handgun belonging to Terry Fisher," Tucker observed, looking up at Daniels. "His fiancée told us she informed Detective Bradley that Terry had acquired a gun shortly before his death, supposedly for protection."

Daniels frowned. "I don't know anything about that, sir. I wasn't on the force back then."

"Is there a supplemental evidence log? Something that might have been filed separately?" Tucker pressed.

"Not that I'm aware of," the officer replied. "Everything should be in that box."

Tucker continued searching, but found no reference to the gun Tiffany had mentioned. Either she had lied about informing Detective Bradley, or the information had been deliberately removed from the official record. Given Bradley's statements about being sidelined after pushing the investigation too far, Tucker figured the latter seemed more likely.

Meanwhile, Mallory was reviewing witness statements, occasionally making notes in her small notebook. They worked in methodical silence for over an hour, the only sounds being the rustle of papers and Officer Daniels occasionally shifting in his chair.

When Tucker opened the box containing Cory Robar's case file, he immediately noticed the difference in thoroughness. Where Terry Fisher's investigation had filled a dozen folders with hundreds of pages of documentation, Robar's entire case fit in less than half the space. The autopsy photos showed the same execution-style wounds, and the crime scene was similarly rural, but the follow-up investigation appeared cursory at best.

"Who was the lead detective on the Robar case?" Tucker asked Daniels.

"Detective Mercer," the officer answered. "He retired about five years ago. Moved to Florida, I think."

The pattern continued with the remaining cases. Each subsequent murder received less investigative attention than the one before, despite the obvious similarities in method and location. By the time Tucker reached Freddy Paul's file—the most recent victim—killed just two years earlier—the investigation appeared to consist of little more than basic crime scene processing and a few perfunctory interviews.

"Chief Winson handled the Paul case personally," Daniels volunteered, noticing Tucker's frown. "We were short-staffed at the time."

Tucker made a note of this. The chief's direct involvement in the most recent murder added another dimension to consider.

After nearly three hours of review, Tucker nodded to Mallory. They had extracted what they could from the official records.

"We'd like copies of certain documents," Tucker told Daniels, indicating several key pages they'd flagged.

"I'll need to get approval from the chief," Daniels replied, looking uncertain.

"It's standard procedure when working with a private investigator on a cold case," Tucker assured him, maintaining a professional tone despite his frustration. "Just the autopsy reports, crime scene photos, and witness statements. Nothing that would compromise any ongoing investigation."

Daniels hesitated, then nodded. "I'll check with the chief and let you know."

As they prepared to leave, Tucker studied the young officer. "How long have you been with the department, Officer Daniels?"

"Three years, sir."

"And you're familiar with these cases?"

Daniels shifted his weight. "Only what I've heard around the station. They're... not really discussed much."

"Five unsolved murders in a small town, all with the same MO, and they're not discussed?" Mallory asked, her tone making it clear how unlikely she found this.

"It's just... it's sensitive," Daniels replied, looking uncomfortable. "Chief Winson prefers we focus on current cases, things we can actually solve."

Tucker nodded, catching the implication. "Thank you for your assistance today, Officer Daniels. We'll be in touch about those copies."

11

Outside in the parking lot, they paused by the passenger side door of their vehicle, out of sight of the PD, to discuss their findings.

"There was no mention of the gun anywhere in Fisher's file," Tucker said quietly. "And the investigations get progressively less thorough with each victim."

"I noticed that too," Mallory agreed. "And there's something else. In the witness statements for Terry's case, there's nothing from Tanya Broadbent."

Tucker frowned. "Who's that?"

"She's mentioned briefly in Malik Williams' file as his girl-friend," Mallory explained. "But when I cross-referenced the witness lists from all five cases, her name jumped out. She's the only person who appears in connection with two different victims. She was a waitress at a local café who knew both Malik Williams and Terry Fisher."

"And yet she wasn't formally interviewed in the Fisher case," Tucker noted. "That's an oversight... or a deliberate omission."

"Either way, she should be on our list to interview," Mallory said. "After the pastor."

Tucker checked his watch. "It's almost noon. Let's get lunch, then head to the church. I called this morning and left a message that we'd like to speak with Pastor Pearcy this afternoon."

They found a small sandwich shop a few blocks from the police station and sat down at a table near the back of the room, where they could talk privately. The lunch crowd was just starting to filter in—mostly locals, judging by the familiar greetings exchanged.

"So, what's your assessment after seeing the files?" Tucker asked, keeping his voice low.

Mallory sipped her iced tea before answering. "Deliberate suppression of the investigation. Bradley did a thorough job with Terry's case, but after he was sidelined, each subsequent murder received less and less attention. Almost like they were going through the motions without any real intention of solving them."

Tucker nodded. "And the missing reference to Terry's gun is significant. Tiffany specifically told us she informed Bradley about it."

"Do you think Bradley removed it from the file himself?" Mallory questioned. "Maybe to protect Tiffany somehow?"

Tucker considered this. "It's possible," he replied, "but unlikely given his reputation for thoroughness. More likely it was removed later, perhaps after his 'accident' and reassignment. Yeah, and I'd like to know more about that accident. I wonder if we should talk to his wife."

"She's passed," Mallory said. "I checked. But, if you're right, it must have been removed by someone who wanted to eliminate any connection to gunrunning, right?"

They ate quickly, discussing their next steps. Tucker's phone vibrated with a text message. The pastor was available to meet them at one-thirty.

The sun was shining on Whitehaven Baptist Church when they arrived. The sign out front announced not only the Sunday services and Wednesday prayer meetings, but also a quote from Proverbs: "The fear of the Lord is the beginning of wisdom."

Tucker parked in the small lot beside the church, noting the well-maintained grounds and fresh paint. Whatever its other secrets, Duckwood clearly supported its house of worship financially.

"Kind of appropriate, don't you think?" Tucker asked, nodding at the sign as they walked toward the front entrance.

Mallory smiled and nodded.

"Over here," a middle-aged woman called from a side entrance.

She introduced herself as Mrs. Larson, the church secretary. "And you must be Mr. Randall and Miss Carver," she said. "Pastor Henry is expecting you. Please follow me." And she led them down a hallway to an office. "He's just finishing up his sermon notes for Sunday."

The pastor's office was surprisingly austere, given the church's prosperous appearance: a simple desk, bookshelves filled with theological texts, and a small seating area with worn but clean furniture. The only decoration was a large wooden cross on the wall and framed photos of what appeared to be mission trips to developing countries.

Pastor Henry Pearcy rose to greet them as they entered. He was tall and lean, with silver hair and piercing blue eyes that suggested intelligence and intensity. Tucker estimated him to be in his late fifties or early sixties, though he moved with the energy of a younger man.

"Mr. Randall, Ms. Carver. How nice to see you," he said and extended his hand to each of them. "Mrs. Larson said you're investigating Terry Fisher's death. I'm so pleased to hear that.

Please, sit down. Can I get you something? Water perhaps. Mrs. Larson makes the best iced tea."

"Not for me, thank you," Tucker said as he sat down on one of the two chairs in front of the desk.

"I'm fine, thank you," Mallory said as she sat down next to him.

Tucker assessed the pastor as they settled into their chairs. There was a quiet authority about him, the practiced ease of someone accustomed to being listened to and respected.

"Thank you for agreeing to meet with us, Pastor," Tucker began. "As you may have heard, we're private investigators working on behalf of the Fisher family. We understand you knew Terry well."

"Yes, that's true. I know all the Fisher family," Pearcy replied, his voice deep and resonant, a preacher's voice, designed to carry to the back pews. "Terry attended our church regularly until his tragic death. His parents also until their health declined. I visit them weekly now, bringing communion and comfort."

"You also conducted Terry's funeral service," Mallory noted.

Pearcy nodded solemnly. "One of the most difficult services I've ever led. A young man cut down in his prime, about to be married, full of promise. The community was shocked."

"We understand you also conducted funeral services for Cory Robar, Samuel Jenkins, Malik Williams, and Freddy Paul," Tucker said, watching the pastor's reaction closely.

If Pearcy was surprised by this direct connection, he hid it well. "Yes, that's correct. All tragic losses to our community."

"All murdered in exactly the same way as Terry Fisher," Mallory added.

"God's ways are indeed mysterious to behold," Pearcy replied, his expression somber. "But evil is real in this world of ours, as any pastor can attest."

Tucker shifted tactics. "We visited the site where Terry's body was found. Detective Bradley referred to it as 'Pearcy's land,' but the official reports list it as the Parsons' farm."

"A common misunderstanding," Pearcy explained smoothly. "The Parsons own the property, but our church has leased a portion of it for over twenty years for our annual revival meetings and summer youth camps. Some locals have taken to calling it 'the church land' or 'Pearcy's field.' It's where Terry was found, yes."

"And what about the other victims?" Tucker pressed. "Were they also found on or near this same property?"

The pastor hesitated briefly. "I believe some were in that general vicinity, yes. Duckwood is small, Mr. Randall. Many locations are in relative proximity to each other."

"Five murdered men, all found within a five-mile radius, all killed execution-style, all with funeral services conducted by you," Mallory summarized. "That seems like more than coincidence."

Pearcy's expression remained composed, but Tucker noted a slight tightening around his eyes. "I'm one of only two Baptist pastors in Duckwood, Ms. Carver. Most local families from this end of town attend our church, or at least turn to us in times of crisis. It's not unusual that I would be called upon to provide funeral services."

"Did you know all five men personally?" Tucker asked.

"To varying degrees," Pearcy replied. "Terry better than the others, of course. Cory attended services occasionally. The others, less so, though I had met each of them through community events or mutual acquaintances."

"Did any of them ever confide in you about being involved in or witnessing illegal activities?" Tucker asked directly. "Gunrunning, for instance?"

The pastor's calm demeanor slipped for just a moment—a

flash of something in his eyes that might have been anger or fear —before his professional mask returned.

"I'm afraid I can't discuss what may have been shared in pastoral confidence," he said, his tone cooling slightly. "But I can assure you that if any of these men had come to me with knowledge of serious crimes, I would have encouraged them to go straight to the proper authorities."

"Even if those authorities might have been compromised?" Mallory suggested.

Pearcy's gaze sharpened. "That's a serious allegation, Ms. Carver. Our local police department serves this community with dedication and integrity."

Tucker decided to take a different approach. "We're not making accusations, Pastor. We're simply trying to understand why five men would be murdered in the same manner in a small town like this over the course of eleven years, with seemingly no progress in any of the investigations."

"Sometimes evil goes unpunished in this life," Pearcy replied, his voice taking on a preacher's cadence. "But rest assured, God's justice is inevitable, if not always immediate."

"We're more concerned with earthly justice at the moment," Tucker said evenly. "For the families who have lost loved ones."

The pastor nodded, his expression softening. "As am I, Mr. Randall. The Fisher family has suffered greatly, and I pray daily for their comfort and for a resolution to this tragedy. It's good that you're here. I will pray to God that you're successful."

"One more question," Mallory said. "Do you know Tanya Broadbent? She worked as a waitress at a local café and was dating Malik Williams when he was killed."

Something flickered across Pearcy's face: recognition, certainly, but it might also have been concern.

"Yes, I know Tanya," he acknowledged. "A troubled young woman with a difficult past. She came to our church a few times after Malik's death, seeking comfort. I haven't seen her in some months, though."

"Do you know where we might find her?" Tucker asked.

Pearcy hesitated. "I believe she lives in a small house near the lake. Green siding, on Lakeview Drive. But I'd approach carefully if I were you. Tanya has struggled with... substances... over the years. Her perspective may not be entirely reliable."

Tucker noted the warning; similar to ones they'd received about Detective Bradley. It seemed everyone in Duckwood was eager to discredit potential witnesses before they could even speak.

As they prepared to leave, Pearcy rose and extended his hand again. "I hope you find the answers you're seeking. For the Fishers' sake, and for all the families who have lost loved ones."

"Thank you for your time, Pastor," Tucker replied, shaking his hand firmly. "We may have additional questions as our investigation progresses."

"My door is always open," Pearcy assured them, though his smile didn't quite reach his eyes. "God bless you both, and your efforts."

Back in the car, Tucker and Mallory processed the conversation in silence for a moment before Mallory spoke.

"He definitely knows more than he's saying."

Tucker nodded, starting the engine. "That's a given," he said. "The question is, though, whether he's involved directly or simply protecting information shared in confidence."

"Did you notice how he reacted when I mentioned Tanya Broadbent? That was more than just recognition."

"Yes, I caught that, too," Tucker agreed. "Let's go find this Tanya Broadbent. If she knew both Terry and Malik, she might be the connection we've been looking for."

As they drove toward Lakeview Drive, Tucker pondered their conversation with the pastor. Pearcy had been polished, controlled, revealing little beyond what was necessary. But there had been moments—brief lapses in his composed facade—that suggested deeper knowledge of the events surrounding the murders.

Whether that knowledge made him a witness, an accessory, or something else entirely remained to be seen. But Tucker's instincts told him that Pastor Henry Pearcy was a key piece in the puzzle they were assembling—a puzzle that someone in Duckwood was willing to kill to keep unsolved.

The lake area was more upscale than the rest of Duckwood, with newer homes and well-maintained properties taking advantage of the water views. Lakeview Drive curved along the shoreline, featuring a mix of year-round residences and summer cabins.

"Green siding," Mallory reminded him, scanning the houses they passed.

Tucker spotted it first—an older, small, somewhat neglected house set back from the road, its green paint faded and peeling in places. A ten-year-old blue sedan was parked in the gravel driveway, and a set of wind chimes hung from the small front porch.

"That must be it," he said, pulling over a short distance away. "Let's approach carefully. If she knew two of the victims, she might be wary of strangers asking questions."

They walked up to the house together, Tucker slightly ahead. The porch steps creaked under their weight as they approached the front door. Tucker knocked firmly, listening for movement inside.

Nothing.

He knocked again, louder this time. Still no response.

Mallory peered through a front window, then shook her head. "I don't see anyone moving inside."

Tucker tried the doorknob—it was locked, as expected. They

circled the small house, checking windows and calling Tanya's name. The back door was secured as well, and there was no sign of forced entry or struggle.

"She could be at work," Mallory suggested. "Or running errands."

Tucker nodded, but a sense of unease was growing in his gut. "Let's check with the neighbors, see if anyone knows when she was last seen."

The nearest house was about fifty yards away, a better-maintained property with flower beds and a boat in the driveway. An elderly man was watering plants near the road as they approached.

"Excuse me, sir," Tucker called. "We're looking for Tanya Broadbent. Do you know if she's home?"

The man turned, regarding them suspiciously. "Who's asking?"

Tucker introduced themselves as private investigators, explaining they needed to speak with Tanya about a case they were working on.

The man's expression changed from suspicion to something like concern. "I haven't seen Tanya in a couple days. Not unusual, though. She keeps to herself mostly. She works odd shifts at the café."

"Has she lived here long?" Mallory asked.

"Bout three years," the man replied. "Rents the place from Carl Parsons, the same fella who owns the farm where they found that Fisher boy's body years back." He peered at them more closely. "That what you're investigating? Those murders?"

"We can't discuss the details," Tucker said diplomatically. "But if you see Tanya, could you ask her to call us?" He offered a business card, which the man accepted reluctantly and then stared at it.

"You folks be careful," the neighbor warned, glancing toward

Tanya's house. "Strange things happen around here sometimes. People who ask too many questions about those killings tend to regret it."

It was the third such warning they'd received since arriving in Duckwood. Tucker was beginning to think it was less coincidence and more orchestrated intimidation.

"We'll keep that in mind," he assured the man. "Thank you for your help."

As they walked back to their SUV, Mallory leaned close. "Another connection to the Parsons property," she murmured. "And another missing witness."

Tucker nodded grimly. "Let's check the café, see if she's working today. And if not..."

"If not, we might need to be concerned about her safety," Mallory finished his thought.

The pieces were coming together, but the picture they formed was increasingly disturbing. Five murdered men. Missing evidence. Witnesses who couldn't or wouldn't talk. And now, potentially, another victim.

Whatever secrets Duckwood was hiding, they were worth killing for. And Tucker had the growing conviction that he and Mallory had stumbled into something far more dangerous than a simple cold case investigation.

12

MALLORY SCANNED THE BUSY INTERIOR OF MOLLY'S CAFÉ, searching for Tanya Broadbent among the waitstaff. The afternoon crowd filled most of the tables—a mix of locals having coffee and tourists passing through. A server—middle-aged with tired eyes and a harried look—approached their table.

"Help you folks?" she asked, order pad ready.

"We're looking for Tanya Broadbent," Mallory replied. "Does she work today?"

The waitress's expression shifted subtly, a flicker of something that might have been concern. "Tanya? No, she hasn't been in for her shifts the last two days. And it's not like her to miss without calling. You friends of hers?"

"We needed to speak with her about an investigation," Tucker explained, showing his PI credentials discreetly. "Do you know where we might find her?"

The waitress—Sally, according to her nametag—glanced around before leaning closer. "Look, Tanya's had a rough go of it. After what happened to Malik, she was pretty broken up. Started asking questions nobody around here wants answered."

"Questions about his murder?" Mallory pressed.

Sally nodded. "She said she had theories about who was behind it, why he was killed. Most folks just thought she was messed up from grief and, well, other issues." She tapped her temple meaningfully. "But lately she seemed clearer, said she had proof of something. Then she just stops showing up."

Mallory felt her pulse quicken. "When exactly did you last see her?"

"Monday morning. She worked the breakfast shift, left around two o'clock." Sally paused. "The strange thing is, she seemed excited. She said she finally had what she needed to 'blow it all open,' whatever that means."

Today was Wednesday. Tanya had been missing, or at least unreachable, for almost two days, right around the time they'd arrived in Duckwood.

"Did she mention what kind of proof she had?" Tucker asked.

Sally shook her head. "Tanya talked big sometimes, especially when she'd been drinking. But she seemed different this time. More... I dunno, certain." She hesitated, then added, "You might try Louis Fisher. They were kinda friendly."

"Louis Fisher?" Mallory repeated, surprised. "Terry's cousin? Tiffany's husband?"

"That's him. He'd stop by the café when Tanya was working, sit at the counter, talking with her. Nothing inappropriate. It just seemed like they had some kind of understanding, like, you know?"

Mallory exchanged a glance with Tucker. This was an unexpected connection—Louis Fisher, who had married Terry's fiancée, was also friendly with a woman connected to another victim.

"One more question," Mallory said. "Do you know if Tanya knew Terry Fisher before his death?"

Sally's eyebrows rose. "Terry? Yeah, they knew each other.

They grew up together. Dated briefly in high school before he got with Tiffany. Why?"

This was significant, a direct personal connection between Tanya and both victims. "Oh," Mallory said, shaking her head. "No, I'm just... trying to establish connections. Thank you so much for your help."

They ordered coffee to avoid drawing attention, waiting until Sally moved away before discussing what they'd learned.

"So Tanya dated Terry in high school, then later dated Malik, another victim," Mallory summarized quietly. "And she's friendly with Louis Fisher, who married Terry's fiancée after his death."

"And now she's missing after claiming to have proof of something," Tucker added. "We need to find her. And we need to speak with Louis Fisher."

"I'll check social media for any recent activity from Tanya," Mallory suggested, pulling out her phone. "You try Gary; see if he knows where his cousin might be."

While Tucker stepped outside to make the call, Mallory searched for Tanya Broadbent online. She found a Facebook profile that hadn't been updated in months and an Instagram with occasional posts of nature photos and inspirational quotes. Nothing that indicated where she might be or what "proof" she might have discovered.

Tucker returned as she was scrolling through Tanya's sparse social media presence. "Gary says Louis works at the hardware store on Main Street. Should be there until six o'clock today."

"Anything else?"

"Gary seemed surprised we were asking about Louis. Said they're not close since Louis married Tiffany, but as far as he knows, Louis is a straight arrow; works hard, attends church, coaches Little League."

"And apparently has secret conversations with a woman connected to two murder victims," Mallory added.

They paid for their coffee and left, deciding to drive past Tanya's house once more before approaching Louis. The small green house looked exactly as they'd left it: quiet, seemingly unoccupied, with no new signs of activity.

"I'm getting worried," Mallory admitted as they pulled away. "The timing is too coincidental. She discovers some kind of proof as to what happened to Malik, then disappears right when we arrive in town and start asking questions."

"Let's not jump to conclusions," Tucker said, though she could see by his expression he was equally concerned. "But let's find Louis Fisher and see what he knows," he said.

THE GOODMAN HARDWARE Store was a local institution, judging by the worn but well-maintained facade and the "Serving Our Community Since 1952" sign in the window. Inside, the narrow aisles were packed with everything from paint supplies to fishing gear, the smell of sawdust and metal permeating the air.

A young clerk directed them to the back, where a man in his early forties was cutting keys for a customer. Louis Fisher was broader than his cousin Gary, with a solid build and calloused hands that spoke of physical work. His brown hair was neatly trimmed, his expression pleasant as he handed the keys to the customer with a friendly comment.

Tucker and Mallory waited until the customer left before approaching. "Mr. Fisher? Louis Fisher?" Tucker began. "We'd like to speak with you if you have a moment."

Louis looked up, his expression curious but not alarmed. "That's me. What can I help you with?"

"I'm Tucker Randall, and this is Mallory Carver. We're

private investigators working with Gary Fisher regarding his brother's murder."

The change in Louis was subtle but immediate: a stiffening of his shoulders, a slight narrowing of his eyes. "Gary hired private investigators? He didn't mention that."

"It was a recent decision," Mallory explained, observing his reactions. "Given his parents' declining health, he's hoping for a solution before it's too late."

Louis nodded slowly. "Understandable. Though I'm not sure what I can tell you that the police haven't already covered. Terry died long before Tiffany and I got together."

There was a defensiveness in his tone that caught Mallory's attention—as if he expected to be judged for marrying his murdered cousin's fiancée.

"Actually, we're hoping you might help us locate someone," Tucker said. "Tanya Broadbent. We understand you know her."

Louis' expression shifted again to one of surprise, followed by something that might have been concern. "Tanya? Why would you need to find her?"

"She knew both Terry and Malik Williams," Mallory explained. "We believe she might have information relevant to our investigation."

"Have you checked Molly's café?" he asked. "She works there."

"She hasn't shown up for her shifts in two days," Tucker replied. "Her house appears empty, and no one seems to know where she is."

Louis ran a hand through his hair, a gesture that reminded Mallory of Gary. The family resemblance was stronger in movement than appearance. "That's... concerning. Tanya's had her struggles, but she's reliable about work."

"When did you last see her?" Mallory asked.

Louis hesitated, his gaze flicking between them. "Monday

evening. She stopped by the house briefly to drop off a book she'd borrowed from Tiffany."

"Did she seem distracted in any way? Excited, worried, afraid?"

"Not that I noticed," Louis replied, but there was a slight delay in his response that made Mallory doubt his sincerity. "Look, why all these questions about Tanya? What does she have to do with Terry's murder?"

"We're exploring all the avenues," Tucker said smoothly. "Tanya dated Terry in high school, then later dated Malik Williams; both were murdered in identical fashion. That makes her perspective potentially valuable. We need to speak with her."

Louis's eyebrows rose. "I knew she'd dated Malik, but Terry? That's news to me." He paused. "Does Tiffany know you're investigating all this again? She's worked hard to move forward with her life."

"We've spoken with Tiffany," Mallory confirmed. "She mentioned Terry had acquired a gun shortly before his death, supposedly for protection. Did he ever discuss that with you?"

Louis's expression closed off further. "No. Terry and I weren't especially close back then. Different circles, different interests." He glanced at his watch. "Look, I need to get back to work. Is there anything else?"

Tucker handed him a business card. "If you hear from Tanya, please let us know immediately. We're concerned about her safety."

Louis took the card reluctantly. "Sure. Though Tanya sometimes goes off-grid when she's having a rough patch. She might just be taking some personal time."

As they turned to leave, Mallory paused. "One more question, Mr. Fisher. Do you know Pastor Henry Pearcy well?"

"Pastor Henry?" Louis seemed surprised by the shift. "Of

course. He's our pastor. He conducted Terry's funeral, counseled Tiffany after his death, and he performed our wedding ceremony. Why?"

"Just establishing connections," Mallory replied with a smile. "Thank you for your time, Mr. Fisher."

Outside, they walked a block before discussing the interview, wary of being overheard.

"He's hiding something," Mallory stated confidently. "That business about Tanya returning a book to Tiffany? I don't buy it. Tiffany never mentioned being friends with her."

Tucker nodded. "And he seemed genuinely surprised that Tanya had dated Terry. If they were as friendly as the waitress suggested, wouldn't that have come up?"

"We need to find Tanya," Mallory said, feeling increasingly uneasy about the woman's absence. "If she had proof of something related to the murders, and now she's missing..."

"Let's check with the police first," Tucker suggested. "File a missing person report, make it official. If something has happened to her, we want a paper trail documenting our concerns."

13

THE DUCKWOOD POLICE DEPARTMENT WAS QUIET WHEN THEY returned. The receptionist from that morning replaced by a young male officer. He looked up as they entered, recognition flickering in his eyes.

"You're the private investigators, right? How can I help you?"

Tucker explained their concerns about Tanya Broadbent, her missed work shifts, the empty house, her claims of having proof related to the murders they were investigating.

The officer—Peters, according to his nameplate—typed notes into his computer as they spoke, but Mallory noted his lack of urgency. "So she's been missing since Monday afternoon?" he asked. "That's not very long. Adults are entitled to go wherever they want without reporting in."

"Under normal circumstances, yes," Mallory agreed. "But given the context, her connection to two murder victims, her claim to have evidence, and the threatening note we received after asking questions about those same murders, we believe there's cause for concern."

Officer Peters looked uncomfortable. "I'll file the report and pass it along to the chief. But without signs of foul play or a much longer absence, there's not much we can do officially."

"We understand," Tucker said. "We'd just like our concerns documented. And we'd appreciate being notified if she turns up."

After completing the paperwork, they left the station, both frustrated by the lukewarm response but not surprised.

"They're not going to look for her," Mallory said as they walked to their vehicle. "At least not seriously."

"Which means it's up to us," Tucker agreed. "But where do we start? We've checked her home, her workplace. No one seems to know where she might go."

Mallory considered the puzzle pieces they'd collected. "The waitress said Tanya claimed to have proof. What if she didn't just discover something? What if she went somewhere to get that proof?"

"Like where?"

"The Parsons' farm," Mallory suggested. "It's where Terry's body was found, and apparently where the church holds events. Tanya even rents her house from Carl Parsons. Those are connections, but there's something we're missing."

Tucker nodded slowly. "It's worth checking out, I suppose. But we should wait until dark. If someone's watching us—and that note suggests they are—we don't want to telegraph our movements."

They decided to return to their hotel to review their notes and plan their approach to the Parsons property. As they drove, Mallory's phone rang. It was her sister, Jen, again.

"I should take this," she sighed, answering the call. "Hey, Jen."

"Please tell me you're heading back tomorrow," Jen said without preamble. "The dress appointment is at two on Friday, and I've already had to reschedule twice."

"I'm not sure," Mallory admitted, glancing at Tucker. "Things are getting complicated here."

Jen was quiet for a moment. "Mal, I know your work is important. But so is your wedding. And your safety. Maybe you should let the local police handle the investigation."

Mallory suppressed a bitter laugh. "The local police aren't exactly eager to investigate anything. That's part of the problem."

They talked a few minutes longer, with Mallory promising to call the next day with a definite answer about the dress appointment. When she hung up, Tucker gave her a sympathetic glance.

"You should go back for that appointment if you want," he offered. "I told you, I can handle things here for a day."

Mallory shook her head firmly. "Not with Tanya missing and the case heating up. The dress can wait."

Back at the hotel, they spread their notes across Tucker's bed and began creating a timeline of events and connections between the various players in Duckwood.

"So we have five victims over eleven years, all killed the same way," Tucker summarized. "Terry Fisher, who was engaged to Tiffany, who later married his cousin Louis. Terry dated Tanya in high school. Years later, Tanya dated Malik Williams, another victim."

"And apparently Tanya and Louis were friendly recently, despite there being no obvious reason for them to interact," Mallory added. "Pastor Pearcy conducted all five funeral services and leases the land where Terry's body was found from the Parsons family, who also happen to be Tanya's landlord."

"Then there's the gunrunning operation that Detective Bradley was investigating before his accident," Tucker said. "And the gun that Terry acquired shortly before his death, which mysteriously disappeared from the case files."

Mallory stood and paced the small room, trying to see the

connections more clearly. "What if the gunrunning operation is the key to everything? Say Terry somehow got involved, or discovered it, then was killed before he could expose it. The other victims followed the same pattern. Say they knew something, threatened exposure, and were eliminated?"

"Possible, and what about Tanya?" Tucker prompted.

"Maybe she finally figured it out. Maybe she found evidence of who's behind it all." Mallory paused by the window, lifting the edge of the curtain to peer outside. "That's why we need to check the Parsons property. If there's some kind of operation centering on that land, there might be physical evidence: a building, equipment, something that would explain why five bodies were found in that same general area."

Tucker checked his watch. "It's almost seven. We should get dinner, then wait until after dark to check out the property."

They chose a different restaurant for dinner, a small Italian place off the main street where Tucker figured they'd be less likely to encounter people they'd already interviewed. Over pasta, they continued refining their theory, keeping their voices low and watching for anyone paying them undue attention.

"Even if we find evidence of gunrunning," Tucker pointed out, "we'll need to determine who's behind it. Is it the Parsons family? Pastor Pearcy? Chief Winson? Or some combination of all three?"

"Or someone we haven't even considered yet," Mallory added. "Duckwood might be small, but there are still plenty of people we haven't spoken with."

By the time they finished dinner, darkness had fallen. They returned to their hotel room briefly to change into darker clothing and gather flashlights and weapons, then they headed out toward the Parsons property.

14

Once they left the main road, Tucker drove with the headlights dimmed, following a winding country lane that led toward the area where Terry's body had been discovered. They passed occasional houses set back from the road, but the properties grew larger and more isolated as they continued onward.

"The main farmhouse should be up ahead," Tucker said quietly, referring to the map they'd studied. "We'll park well back and approach on foot."

Mallory felt the familiar mixture of tension and excitement that accompanied potentially dangerous investigative work. Her hand instinctively checked the pepper spray in her pocket and the Sig P938 she carried by habit. Tucker, she knew, carried a Glock 17 in a holster on his belt and a small Smith and Wesson revolver in an ankle holster, a habit from his FBI days that had proven useful more than once.

They parked in a small turnoff hidden by trees, then began the half-mile walk toward the Parsons property. The night was clear but moonless; the darkness broken only by distant porch lights and the glow of their carefully shielded flashlights.

"Terry's body was found in that field to the east of the main farm buildings," Tucker whispered as they approached. "The area where the church holds its events."

Mallory nodded, scanning the landscape. The silhouette of a large barn was visible ahead with what appeared to be equipment sheds and the main farmhouse some distance away. No lights burned in any of the buildings.

"Let's check the barn first," she suggested. "It's the most logical place to store or transfer illegal goods."

They moved silently across the open ground, staying low and using the sparse tree line for cover when possible. As they neared the barn, Mallory noticed something that made her pause—fresh tire tracks in the dirt driveway, despite there being no vehicles visible.

"Someone's been here recently," she whispered to Tucker, indicating the tracks.

He nodded, eyes alert as they continued toward the barn. The massive door was secured with a padlock, but a smaller side entrance stood slightly ajar. Tucker approached it cautiously, listening for any sound from inside before slowly pushing it open.

The interior was pitch black. Tucker clicked on his flashlight, keeping the beam low and sweeping it across the concrete floor. Farm equipment filled much of the space: tractors, attachments, tools hanging on the walls. Nothing immediately suspicious.

They moved deeper into the barn, checking behind equipment and scanning for anything out of place. Mallory was beginning to think they'd made a mistake when her beam caught something reflective in the far corner—a tarp covering what appeared to be crates.

"Tucker," she whispered, pointing.

They approached carefully, Tucker taking the lead while Mallory watched their backs. He lifted the edge of the tarp, revealing a stack of wooden crates with foreign markings.

"Military-grade weapons shipping containers," he murmured, recognizing the markings from his FBI training. "Russian manufacturer."

Mallory felt a surge of vindication. "So the gunrunning operation is real. These must be in transit to somewhere else."

Tucker was about to respond when a sound from outside froze them both—the crunch of tires on gravel, headlights sweeping across the barn walls through cracks in the siding.

"Someone's coming," Mallory whispered urgently. "We need to hide."

They quickly replaced the tarp and moved behind a large tractor, crouching low as vehicle doors slammed outside. Voices approached—at least two men, maybe more.

The side door creaked open wider, flashlight beams cutting through the darkness. Mallory pressed closer to Tucker, her heart pounding as footsteps entered the barn.

"Let's make this quick," a man's voice said, his tone authoritative and vaguely familiar. "The shipment needs to be on the road by midnight."

"What about the woman?" another voice asked. "Pearcy says she's asking too many questions."

"She's contained for now," a third voice said. "We'll deal with her after the shipment's gone."

Mallory felt her blood run cold. The woman had to be Tanya. And if she was "contained," it meant she was alive—for now.

Tucker's hand found hers in the darkness, squeezing once in silent communication. They were outnumbered, potentially outgunned, and had stumbled into the middle of an active illegal operation. Their only advantage was that they hadn't been discovered... yet.

The men moved toward the crates, unaware of the investigators hiding behind the tractor.

Tucker remained perfectly still behind the tractor, controlling his breathing as the men moved about the barn. Years of FBI training had prepared him for situations like this: discovery meant danger, not just for him and Mallory, but also for Tanya Broadbent, who was apparently being held somewhere.

He counted the footsteps, trying to determine exactly how many men had entered. Three, possibly four. Their flashlight beams swept across the barn's interior, illuminating dusty farm equipment and the covered crates in the corner.

"Start loading them now," the authoritative voice commanded. "Truck's waiting on the north access road."

"What about those investigators asking around town?" another man asked, his tone betraying nervousness. "Pearcy said they filed a report about the Broadbent woman."

Tucker felt Mallory tense beside him at the mention of the report.

The authoritative voice replied with a dismissive snort.

"Winson will handle that. Small-town PI's from Chattanooga; they're nothing to worry about. Focus on getting this shipment out. We've got buyers waiting."

The sound of the tarp being pulled back echoed in the cavernous space, followed by the scraping of crates being moved. Tucker carefully shifted position to peer through a gap in the tractor's machinery. Four men were visible now, working methodically to load the wooden crates onto hand trucks.

One man, whose face remained in shadow, appeared to be supervising rather than assisting with the physical labor. From his stature and the deference the others showed him, Tucker assumed he was the leader, and the source of the authoritative voice.

Tucker reached down slowly to the Glock 17 on his belt, confirming his weapon was accessible if needed. He had no intention of engaging in a firefight while outnumbered, but if they were discovered, having options might make the difference between life and death.

The loading continued for several minutes; the men working efficiently in near silence. Tucker noted their practiced movements. These men weren't amateurs; they were people who had done this many times before. The operation was clearly well-established, explaining why it had continued uninterrupted for over a decade.

"Last one," one of the men announced, loading a final crate.

"Good," the leader replied. "Meet at the rendezvous in thirty minutes. I need to check on our guest first."

Guest. Tucker exchanged a glance with Mallory in the darkness. That had to be Tanya. If they followed the leader, he might lead them right to her.

The men began moving toward the door, taking the loaded hand trucks with them. Tucker calculated rapidly—they needed to avoid detection but not lose their chance to find Tanya. He leaned close to Mallory's ear.

"Stay here until they're gone," he whispered, barely audible. "I'll follow at a distance. Wait five minutes, then return to the car."

She gave a nearly imperceptible nod, though he could sense her reluctance to separate. But it was the safest approach—one person trailing was less likely to be detected than two, and if something went wrong, Mallory would be free to contact authorities.

15

As the men exited the barn, Tucker counted to thirty, then carefully moved from their hiding place toward the door. The night outside seemed to have grown darker, clouds now obscuring what little starlight had illuminated their approach. He could see flashlight beams moving away toward different vehicles—two heading north, presumably with the weapons, and one moving west, toward what appeared to be a smaller outbuilding about a hundred yards from the barn.

Tucker slipped out the side door and pressed himself against the barn's exterior wall, using the shadows for cover. The leader was walking alone toward the outbuilding, his flashlight bobbing with each step. Tucker waited until there was sufficient distance, then began following, moving from shadow to shadow, careful to avoid making a noise on the gravel and dirt.

The outbuilding appeared to be a storage shed, perhaps twenty feet square, with a metal roof. Unlike the barn, it had a sturdy-looking door with what appeared to be a modern electronic lock. The leader approached it, his flashlight illuminating a keypad mounted beside the door. Tucker watched from behind a stack of hay bales as the man punched in a code, the lock disengaging with an audible click.

The door opened, spilling light from inside onto the ground. The leader entered, closing the door behind him. Tucker moved closer, circling to approach from the side where a small window might offer visibility inside. Crouching beneath it, he slowly raised his head just enough to peer inside.

The shed's interior had been converted into a makeshift holding cell. A camp bed stood against one wall, and a woman he assumed was Tanya Broadbent sat on it, her hands bound in front of her but her feet free. She appeared disheveled but uninjured, her expression defiant as she faced the leader, who was now illuminated in the overhead light.

Tucker felt a jolt of recognition. The leader was Carl Parsons, owner of the farm, Tanya's landlord, and a man whose name had repeatedly surfaced during their investigation, a man whose photograph he'd seen several times during his research.

He was speaking to Tanya, his tone was condescending. Tucker put his ear to the glass.

"...just need to cooperate, and this ends well for everyone. Where's the evidence you claimed to have?"

"Go to hell," Tanya spat back. "I know what you did to Malik. To Terry. To all of them."

Parsons sighed, as if dealing with a troublesome child. "We've been through this, Tanya. You have theories, not evidence. If you had actual proof, you would have produced it by now."

"Maybe I already gave it to someone for safekeeping," she countered. "Maybe if anything happens to me, it goes straight to the state police."

Tucker couldn't see Parsons' face from his angle, but the man's posture stiffened. "You're bluffing. There's no one in Duckwood you trust enough for that."

"Who said anything about anyone in Duckwood?" she snapped.

The statement hung in the air between them. Tucker recognized the strategy. Tanya was trying to create doubt, to make her captors hesitate before doing anything permanent. It was a smart play, but she was clearly in serious danger.

Tucker weighed his options. He was armed, but engaging in a direct confrontation with Parsons now could put Tanya at greater risk. He needed to get back to Mallory, formulate a plan, and call in reinforcements—though given Chief Winson's apparent involvement in the conspiracy, the local police weren't an option, and neither could he assume the sheriff wasn't involved.

He carefully backed away from the window, keeping low and using the ambient noise of the rural night to mask any sounds. Once at a safe distance, he circled wide around the buildings, heading back toward where they'd parked. His mind raced with the implications of what he'd witnessed. The gunrunning operation was real, and had been operating for years, and Carl Parsons appeared to be a key figure, perhaps even the leader, though from what had been said in the barn, it was clear that the pastor was also somehow involved.

Halfway back to their parking spot, Tucker heard the soft crunch of footsteps ahead. He froze, hand moving toward his weapon, then relaxed slightly as Mallory's familiar outline emerged from the darkness.

"I told you to wait at the car," he whispered as she approached.

"You know I don't follow instructions well," she replied quietly. "What did you find?"

"Tanya's alive. She's being held in one of the sheds. Carl Parsons is holding her, and he appears to be running the gun operation. We need to get back to the car and call for help."

They moved quickly through the darkness, staying off the main access road and using the tree line for cover. Once they reached their vehicle, Tucker did a quick check to ensure it hadn't been tampered with before they got inside.

"Who do we call?" Mallory asked as Tucker started the engine, keeping the headlights off as they pulled away. "Not the local police, not if Winson is involved somehow."

"State police," Tucker decided, putting distance between them and the Parsons farm before turning on the headlights. "But we need to be careful about what we say. We don't know how far this conspiracy extends."

"Did you hear what he said about the pastor?" Mallory asked.

"Yes, it seems he must be somehow involved, too," he replied as he drove toward the main highway, planning to get well outside Duckwood before making the call. As they rounded a curve in the country road, headlights suddenly appeared behind them, closing fast.

"We've got company," Mallory warned, looking back.

Tucker accelerated, but the pursuing vehicle—a large pickup truck—gained on them rapidly. "Call now," he instructed Mallory, tossing her his phone. "Tennessee Highway Patrol. Tell them we're being pursued and believe it's connected to illegal weapons trafficking."

Mallory went to her contacts and tapped the number while Tucker focused on driving, pushing their small SUV to its limits on the winding rural road. The pickup behind them was now close enough that its headlights filled their rear window, illuminating the interior as bright as day.

"It's ringing," Mallory reported. "Wait—we're losing signal."

Tucker glanced at the phone and saw the "No Service" indicator. "We must be in a dead zone. Keep trying."

The road ahead straightened as they approached the

highway intersection. Tucker accelerated further, hoping to reach the main road where there might be other traffic or better cell reception. The pickup responded in kind, its engine roaring as it closed the gap.

"Hold on," Tucker warned as he took the turn onto the high-way, tires squealing in protest. The pursuing truck followed, now just car lengths behind them. In the side mirror, Tucker could see the driver clearly; it was one of the men from the barn.

"They're going to ram us," Mallory said tensely, bracing herself against the dashboard.

The impact came seconds later; the pickup slammed into their rear bumper, causing their vehicle to fishtail briefly before Tucker regained control. He sped up again, but their vehicle was no match for the more powerful pickup.

Another impact, harder this time, sent them skidding toward the shoulder. Tucker fought the wheel, keeping them on the road, but a third hit knocked them into a spin. The SUV rotated one-hundred-eighty degrees before sliding to a stop on the opposite shoulder, facing back the way they had come.

The pickup braked hard and skidded to a stop some twenty yards away. Its headlights illuminated their disabled vehicle as two men emerged, both carrying what appeared to be handguns.

"Get down," Tucker ordered, drawing his weapon. "When I engage them, run for the trees on your side."

"I'm not leaving you," Mallory protested.

"This isn't a debate. One of us needs to get help." His tone left no room for argument. "Now get ready."

The men approached cautiously, weapons raised. Tucker waited until they were thirty feet away before making his move. He pushed his door open, using it as partial cover while aiming at the closest attacker.

"FBI! Drop your weapons!" he shouted, falling back on his old authority out of instinct.

The men hesitated briefly, just long enough for Tucker to fire a warning shot over their heads. They dove for cover, returning fire almost immediately. Bullets pinged against the SUV's body and shattered the driver's side window.

"Go!" Tucker yelled to Mallory, firing again to provide covering fire as she slipped out the passenger side and sprinted for the tree line.

One of the men noticed her escape and turned to fire in her direction. Tucker adjusted his aim and shot more deliberately this time, hitting the man in the shoulder. He went down with a cry of pain as Mallory disappeared into the darkness beyond the road.

The second attacker unleashed a barrage of bullets, forcing Tucker to duck behind the engine block for cover. He was pinned down now, with limited ammunition and an injured but still armed opponent, plus the second attacker methodically closing in on his position.

"You're just making this worse for yourself," one of the men called out. "We only want the woman. Tell us where she's going, and maybe you get to walk away from this."

Tucker didn't respond, using the moment to assess his options. His position was deteriorating rapidly. The SUV offered some protection, but they would eventually flank him. His best hope was that Mallory had gotten far enough away to find help or signal passing traffic.

A new sound cut through the night, distant sirens, growing louder. Someone had reported the gunfire, or perhaps a passing motorist had seen the confrontation. Either way, it changed the equation.

"Cops are coming," the uninjured attacker said urgently to his partner. "We need to go. Now."

"What about him?" the wounded man asked, gesturing toward Tucker's position with his good arm.

"Leave him. If he's still alive, Winson can deal with him."

Tucker heard them retreating, car doors slamming, and tires squealing as the pickup reversed course and sped away. He remained in position, gun ready, until the vehicle's taillights disappeared into the distance.

Only then did he allow himself to take stock of his own condition. A sharp pain in his left arm suggested he'd been hit, though adrenaline had masked it during the confrontation. Sure enough, blood was soaking through his sleeve from what appeared to be a graze rather than a direct hit.

The sirens were very close now. Tucker holstered his weapon and raised his hands as the first patrol car came into view, its light bar painting the scene in alternating red and blue. He needed to be careful here. If Winson had been alerted, the responding officers might not be friendly.

To his relief, the cruiser had Tennessee Highway Patrol markings rather than local police. Two officers emerged cautiously, weapons drawn.

"On the ground! Hands where we can see them!" one shouted.

Tucker complied immediately, calling out as he did so. "I'm a licensed private investigator. I was just attacked by armed men. My partner fled into the woods for safety."

The officers approached carefully, one keeping him covered while the other checked the immediate area.

"Anyone else here?" the officer asked, holstering his weapon after confirming Tucker was not an immediate threat.

"No, they fled when they heard your sirens. Two men in a dark pickup, one injured. They're connected to an illegal weapons trafficking operation based at the Parsons farm in

Duckwood. And they're holding a woman captive there, Tanya Broadbent."

The officer looked skeptical but radioed the information in while his partner helped Tucker to his feet.

"You're bleeding," the second officer noted, examining Tucker's arm. "We should get you checked out."

"My partner," Tucker insisted. "She ran into those woods. We need to find her first."

"We've got additional units on the way," the officer assured him. "They'll help search for her. Meanwhile, I need your identification and a statement about what happened here."

Tucker provided his PI credentials and gave a concise account of their investigation, the discovery at the Parsons farm, and the subsequent pursuit. He omitted certain details—particularly those that might reveal Mallory's location if she was still hiding—until he could be certain these officers weren't connected to the Duckwood conspiracy.

"This is a serious allegation," the officer said when Tucker had finished. "Weapons trafficking, kidnapping, possible involvement by local law enforcement. We'll need to contact our captain."

"I understand," Tucker replied. "But time is critical. Tanya Broadbent is in immediate danger, and now my partner is missing as well."

The sound of someone emerging from the woods interrupted their conversation. Tucker turned, relief washing over him as he saw Mallory approaching, hands raised to show the officers she wasn't a threat.

"That's my partner," he called out quickly. "Mallory Carver."

The officers verified her identity while Tucker explained what had happened after they separated. Mallory looked shaken but unhurt, her eyes widening at the sight of blood on Tucker's sleeve.

"It's just a graze," he assured her before she could ask. "Did you see which way they went?"

"Back toward Duckwood," she confirmed. "Tucker, I got through to 911 while I was in the woods. State Police dispatch. They're sending units to the Parsons farm."

The highway patrol officer's radio crackled with confirmation. Units were indeed en route to the location, with a warrant being expedited based on the weapons trafficking allegations and suspected kidnapping.

"We need to go there," Tucker insisted. "We can identify Parsons and the shed where Tanya is being held."

The officers exchanged glances. "That's not standard procedure for civilians," the senior officer began.

"We're not civilians," Mallory interjected. "We're licensed investigators who've spent days documenting this case. And he's an ex-FBI agent. We know the layout of the property and can identify the suspects. And every minute we waste puts Tanya in greater danger."

After some discussion over the radio with their supervisor, the officers reluctantly agreed to escort Tucker and Mallory to the Parsons farm, where other units would be converging. An ambulance would meet them there to treat Tucker's wound.

As they drove toward the farm, Tucker's mind raced with contingency plans. If Parsons and his men realized law enforcement was closing in, Tanya might become a liability they couldn't afford to leave alive. And if Chief Winson was alerted before the state police secured the scene, evidence could disappear.

"We found the gunrunning operation," Mallory said quietly beside him in the back of the patrol car. "Just like Detective Bradley suspected eleven years ago."

Tucker nodded. "And likely the motive behind five murders. But we still don't have all the players. Parsons is clearly involved, probably Winson too. But what about Pastor Pearcy? The men at the barn mentioned him."

"One connection at a time," Mallory replied, her hand finding his in the darkness. "Right now, let's focus on saving Tanya."

The patrol car's lights illuminated the rural landscape as they sped toward the Parsons farm. Ahead, Tucker could see the flashing lights of other law enforcement vehicles already on the scene. The operation that had remained hidden for over a decade was about to be exposed—but at what cost?

As they approached, gunfire erupted from the direction of the main farmhouse, answering his question with chilling clarity. The confrontation was far from over.

16

MALLORY TENSED AS MORE GUNFIRE ERUPTED AHEAD. THE Highway Patrol officer driving their cruiser immediately slowed, speaking rapidly into his radio to coordinate with the units already on scene at the Parsons farm.

"Shots fired, multiple officers engaging. All units approach with caution. Civilians present."

Tucker leaned forward. "Any word on the status of the female hostage?"

"Negative," the officer replied, his expression grim. "The team was attempting to clear the outbuildings when they encountered armed resistance."

Mallory's thoughts flew to Tanya, locked in that shed with a firefight raging around her. And she knew if Parsons or his men reached her first, they'd eliminate the witness rather than let her talk.

Their cruiser turned onto the farm's access road, now illuminated by the flashing lights of nearly a dozen police vehicles. Officers in tactical gear had taken positions behind vehicles and outbuildings, their weapons trained on the main farmhouse where muzzle flashes occasionally lit up the windows.

The officer parked well back from the action, turning to his passengers. "You two stay in the vehicle. This is an active shooter situation."

"But the hostage isn't in the main house," Mallory protested. "She's in a storage shed about a hundred yards west of the barn. If you're focusing all your resources on the farmhouse, she's vulnerable."

The officer hesitated, then radioed the information to the command post, which appeared to be set up behind a large SUV with State Police markings. Moments later, a tactical team of four officers detached from the main group and began moving cautiously toward the western outbuildings.

"She's going to be okay," Tucker said quietly, though his expression remained tense. Blood had soaked through the makeshift bandage on his arm, and his face was pale in the flashing lights.

A paramedic approached their vehicle, directed there by one of the officers. "Sir, we need to check that wound."

Tucker reluctantly allowed himself to be guided to a waiting ambulance at the edge of the secured perimeter. Mallory followed, unwilling to let him out of her sight after the close call on the highway.

"It's just a graze," Tucker insisted as the paramedic cut away his sleeve to examine the injury.

"That 'graze' took a chunk of flesh with it," the paramedic countered, cleaning the wound. "You'll need stitches, but it can wait until we get you to a hospital."

"I'm not leaving," Tucker stated firmly. "Not until we find Tanya Broadbent."

The paramedic looked like he wanted to argue, but instead focused on bandaging the wound properly. Mallory stepped a few paces away to speak with the officer in charge, a State Police captain who had approached the ambulance.

"Ms. Carver? I'm Captain Reynolds. I understand you and your partner discovered an illegal weapons operation and a kidnapping victim?"

"Yes," Mallory confirmed, quickly explaining what they'd witnessed in the barn and the shed. "Tucker saw Tanya Broadbent being held by Carl Parsons. She's alive, or was when we left, but in imminent danger."

"We have a team approaching the storage structures now," Reynolds assured her. "Can you describe exactly which building she's in?"

Mallory provided detailed directions to the shed, including the keypad lock she'd glimpsed during their escape. "It's a modern security system; not what you'd expect on a farm storage building."

Reynolds nodded, relaying the information via radio to the tactical team. Meanwhile, the situation at the farmhouse appeared to be escalating. More officers had arrived, including what looked like a SWAT unit from a larger jurisdiction.

"How many hostiles are we dealing with?" Reynolds asked.

"At least four that we saw," Mallory replied. "Parsons and three others. But there could be more."

A burst of radio chatter interrupted them. Reynolds listened intently, then turned back to Mallory, his expression serious.

"The shed's empty. No sign of the hostage."

Mallory felt her stomach drop. "That's impossible. They must have moved her after we left."

"There are signs someone was held there," Reynolds said, "a chair with restraints, some food wrappers. But no hostage."

By then, Tucker had joined them against the paramedic's protests. "They must have relocated her when their men failed to return from pursuing us. Parsons would have realized something went wrong," he said.

Reynolds considered this. "If they moved her, she's likely in the main house now."

"Which complicates your assault," Tucker finished grimly.

The standoff at the farmhouse continued as officers maintained their positions, occasionally exchanging fire with those inside. From their vantage point, Mallory could see tactical officers working their way around the sides of the property, preparing for a coordinated breach.

"We need to get closer," she said to Tucker. "If they bring Tanya out, we're the only ones who can identify her."

"Captain," Tucker addressed Reynolds, "we're both experienced investigators, and I have eight years FBI tactical training. Let us move to your command post where we can assist in identifying the suspects and the hostage."

Reynolds hesitated, then nodded. "Stay behind the vehicles, keep your heads down, and follow my officers' instructions implicitly. Understood?"

They agreed and followed the captain to the SUV serving as the command center. From this new position, they had a clearer view of the farmhouse and the officers surrounding it. A negotiator was attempting to communicate with those inside through a loudspeaker, demanding they release any hostages and surrender.

"Carl Parsons, this is the Tennessee State Police. The building is surrounded. Come out with your hands up and release Tanya Broadbent unharmed."

There was no response except another burst of gunfire from an upstairs window.

"How long has this been going on?" Mallory asked one of the officers manning the radio.

"About twenty minutes," he replied. "They're not responding."

"They know they're cornered," Tucker said. "Men like

Parsons don't surrender easily. They've been operating this gunrunning scheme for over a decade, and they're probably responsible for five murders. They're looking at life sentences."

"Or they're buying time," Mallory suggested, a new thought occurring to her. "Maybe they're waiting for reinforcements."

Tucker looked at her sharply. "You think Winson might show up with local officers?"

"It's possible," she replied. "If he's involved, he can't afford to let Parsons talk."

Captain Reynolds overheard this exchange. "We've notified the County Sheriff's office, not the Duckwood PD. But you're saying the local chief might be corrupt?"

"We have reason to believe Chief Winson is connected to the weapons operation," Tucker confirmed. "And possibly implicated in covering up several murders related to it."

Reynolds' expression hardened. "I'll alert my teams to be cautious about any local law enforcement arriving on scene."

Suddenly, movement at the farmhouse caught Mallory's attention. The front door opened slightly, and someone waved a white cloth.

"They're trying to signal," she said, pointing.

The negotiator immediately responded: "Carl Parsons. Come out slowly with your hands in the air."

Instead of Parsons, a woman was shoved through the doorway, stumbling onto the porch, her hands bound in front of her, squinting in the harsh lights directed at the house. Even from a distance, Mallory was able to recognize Tanya Broadbent.

"That's her," Mallory confirmed to Reynolds. "That's Tanya."

"Hold your fire," Reynolds ordered over the radio. "Female hostage on the porch. Do not engage."

A male voice shouted from inside the house: "We want safe passage! A helicopter to the county airport, or she dies!"

"Standard procedure is not to negotiate transportation,"

Reynolds muttered, then raised the megaphone. "Release the hostage first, then we can discuss terms!"

Tanya stood frozen on the porch, shaking with fear. Then, something unexpected happened. She suddenly dropped to the ground and rolled off the porch into the shadows below, disappearing from the line of fire.

The move caught everyone by surprise, including her captors. Gunfire erupted from the house, spraying wildly in the direction she had fled.

"Covering fire!" Reynolds ordered. "Team Two, extract the hostage!"

Officers responded immediately, laying down suppressing fire while a tactical team rushed forward to retrieve Tanya. Mallory held her breath as the officers reached the area where Tanya had disappeared, then exhaled in relief as they emerged moments later, half-carrying the woman to safety behind the police line.

Tanya was quickly brought to the command post area, where paramedics rushed forward to attend to her. She was disheveled and had bruises on her face and wrists, but otherwise appeared unharmed. Her eyes widened when she saw Mallory and Tucker.

"You're the investigators," she said, her voice hoarse. "You're the reason they were freaking out in there."

"Are you okay?" Mallory asked, kneeling beside her as the paramedics checked her vitals.

"I'll live," Tanya replied grimly. "Better than they're going to."

"How many people are there in the house?" Reynolds asked, kneeling on her other side.

"Three now. Parsons, his son Mike, and a guy named Dunbar who works for them. They've got a stockpile of weapons in there. And they're expecting help."

"From who?" Tucker asked.

Tanya's expression darkened. "Winson. Parsons called him when the police showed up. Said to 'bring everyone' and 'take care of it like before.'"

Reynolds immediately dispatched officers to block the access roads and watch for approaching vehicles.

"What about Pastor Pearcy?" Mallory asked. "The men at the barn mentioned him."

"Pearcy?" Tanya laughed bitterly. "He's as dirty as they come. He's the connection to the buyers. He uses church mission trips as cover to make the arrangements."

"What happened to Terry Fisher? D'you know?" Mallory asked.

"He was involved somehow," she replied. "Exactly how, I don't know."

"So why did they kill him?" Mallory pressed her.

She just shook her head, but didn't reply.

The pieces were falling into place now. "And the others? Cory, Samuel, Malik, Freddy?" Mallory asked. "What about them?"

"Same thing," she replied. "Wrong place, wrong time. They all discovered something they shouldn't. Cory caught them moving guns through the church basement. Malik overheard Parsons and Pearcy talking about a shipment. They eliminate anyone who might expose them."

A fresh barrage of gunfire from the house interrupted their conversation. Reynolds pulled Mallory aside. "We need to move the hostage to safety, and you two as well. We're preparing to breach."

"Wait," Tanya protested, overhearing this. "There's something you need to know. There's evidence—documentation of their entire operation. That's what I found. That's why they grabbed me."

"Where is it?" Tucker asked urgently.

"Hidden at my house. Under the floorboards in my bedroom closet. Names, dates, photos—everything. I've been collecting it for years, ever since they killed Malik."

Reynolds dispatched officers to secure Tanya's residence and retrieve the evidence. Meanwhile, the tactical teams had completed their preparations for breaching the farmhouse.

"We need to clear the area," Reynolds insisted. "This is about to get very active."

Mallory and Tucker followed the officers escorting Tanya toward the medical staging area. As they walked, headlights appeared on the distant access road—multiple vehicles approaching rapidly.

"Incoming!" an officer shouted. "Multiple vehicles, no emergency lights!"

"That'll be Winson," Tucker said grimly, drawing his weapon despite his injured arm.

Reynolds immediately redirected officers to establish a new perimeter facing the approaching vehicles. Mallory, Tucker, and Tanya were hustled behind an armored tactical vehicle for protection as the newcomers arrived at the edge of the police line.

Five Duckwood police cruisers skidded to a stop, and several officers emerged from the first two, including Chief Winson. He approached with an air of authority, apparently unfazed by the state police presence.

"Captain Reynolds? Nate Winson, Duckwood PD. What's the situation here?" His tone was professional, betraying no awareness that his involvement was suspected.

Reynolds met him at the perimeter line. "We have an armed standoff," he replied. "Carl Parsons and two others are barricaded inside, refusing to surrender."

Winson nodded. "I've known Carl for years. Maybe I can talk him down."

"That won't be necessary, Chief," Reynolds replied evenly. "We have the situation under control. In fact, we've already rescued the hostage they were holding."

For the first time, Winson's composed façade cracked slightly. His eyes darted around, eventually landing on Tanya, who was just visible behind the tactical vehicle. Recognition and alarm flickered across his face before he masked it.

"Glad to hear it," he recovered smoothly. "My officers are at your disposal if you need assistance."

"Actually, Chief," Reynolds said, "I'd like you to come with me to discuss something that's come to light during this investigation."

Winson stiffened, his hand drifting subtly toward his sidearm. "What kind of information?"

"It concerns your involvement in an illegal weapons trafficking operation and the cover-up of multiple homicides."

Mallory watched the confrontation tensely, aware that it could go violently wrong in seconds. The Duckwood officers behind Winson looked confused, uncertain whether to follow their chief's lead or stand down.

For a long moment, Winson seemed to calculate his options, his eyes flicking between Reynolds, the state police officers around him, and his own men. Then, with a movement so quick it was almost a blur, he drew his weapon.

"Gun!" someone shouted.

Reynolds reacted instantly, tackling Winson before he could aim. State police officers swarmed forward, subduing the chief while others kept their weapons trained on the Duckwood officers, ordering them to raise their hands.

Most complied immediately, looking shocked at their chief's actions. One younger officer—Daniels, who had supervised their file review—actually stepped forward to help secure

Winson, his expression a mixture of disillusionment and resolve.

"I knew something wasn't right," he said as Reynolds cuffed the struggling chief. "The way those murder cases were handled... it never made any sense."

With Winson secured, attention returned to the farmhouse. The distraction had given the tactical team time to move into final position. Reynolds rejoined them at the command post, leaving Winson in the custody of several officers.

"We're ready to breach," the SWAT commander reported. "On your order, Captain."

Reynolds gave a short nod. "Execute."

The next moments unfolded with the controlled chaos of a tactical operation. Flash-bangs detonated at multiple points inside the farmhouse, followed by the crash of doors and windows being breached simultaneously. Officers poured into the building, shouted commands echoing in the night air.

Gunfire erupted again—a brief, but intense exchange—then silence.

Everyone at the command post waited tensely for the radio to crackle with news. When it finally came, the message was concise:

"Building secure. Two suspects in custody, one deceased. No other casualties."

Mallory exhaled a breath she hadn't realized she'd been holding. Beside her, Tucker's rigid posture relaxed slightly.

"It's over," she said quietly.

"This part is," he agreed. "But we still need to connect all the dots. Parsons, Winson, Pearcy, and any others involved."

"Pearcy," Tanya said suddenly from her seat nearby. "Has anyone gone to the church? He'll know something's wrong by now."

Reynolds overheard and immediately dispatched officers to

locate and detain Pastor Henry Pearcy. But Mallory suspected the pastor was already long gone. Men like him, who maintained respectable facades while orchestrating violence, were usually the first to flee when the operation collapsed.

As the night progressed, the scene transformed from an active tactical situation to a massive crime scene as state evidence technicians arrived to process the farm and its outbuildings. The weapons crates Tucker had discovered earlier were documented and secured. Officers returning from Tanya's house confirmed they'd recovered a substantial cache of evidence hidden exactly where she said it would be.

Tanya herself was transported to the hospital for evaluation, along with two officers assigned to protect her. Before she left, Mallory approached her one last time.

"Thank you," she said simply. "For never giving up on finding the truth."

Tanya looked up at her with tired but determined eyes. "Malik deserved justice," she said. "So did Terry and the others. I couldn't let them get away with it."

"They won't," Mallory assured her. "Not anymore."

As dawn began to lighten the eastern sky, Mallory and Tucker finally allowed themselves to be transported to the hospital. Tucker's arm needed proper medical attention, and they both required treatment for exhaustion and minor injuries sustained during their escape.

In the back of the ambulance, Mallory leaned against Tucker's good shoulder, the adrenaline finally ebbing from her system.

"We did it," she murmured. "We solved five cold case murders in four days."

Tucker put his good arm around her shoulders. "And we exposed a weapons trafficking operation that had corrupted an entire town. Not bad for a couple of private investigators."

"Gary Fisher will finally have answers for his parents," Mallory said, thinking of the family that had waited eleven long years for justice.

"And maybe peace," Tucker added quietly.

As the ambulance wound its way toward the hospital, Mallory felt the weight of the case begin to lift. There would be statements to give, evidence to review, perhaps testimony at trials. But the central mystery—what had happened to Terry Fisher and why—was solved.

Five men had died because of a criminal operation hiding behind the respectable facades of Duckwood. Their killers had believed they could silence the truth forever. But they hadn't counted on the persistence of those left behind; a brother seeking justice and a woman collecting evidence for years.

17

TUCKER SAT ON THE EDGE OF HIS HOSPITAL BED, IMPATIENT TO leave despite the doctor's advice to rest. The wound on his arm had required twelve stitches, and the doctor had warned him about the risk of infection. But there was still work to be done— loose ends to tie up in Duckwood before he could consider the case closed.

Mallory entered the room, tucking her phone away. "Gary Fisher's on his way to see his parents now. He said they've been watching the news coverage all morning."

"It's been on every channel," Tucker said, carefully pulling on his shirt, mindful of his bandaged arm.

"The raid on a gunrunning operation, the arrest of a small-town police chief, five murders solved, it's a big story." Mallory sat beside him. "It's over, Tucker."

"I'm not so sure," Tucker replied, buttoning his shirt one-handed. "We still have work to do."

"What d'you mean, you're not so sure?" she asked, frowning. "What work? Parsons is in custody, Winson too. The state police have the evidence from Tanya's house. We've given our statements."

"Pastor Pearcy is still unaccounted for," Tucker reminded her. "And I want to talk to Louis Fisher again. His connection to Tanya still bothers me."

A knock at the door interrupted them. Captain Reynolds entered, looking tired but satisfied. "I thought I'd find you both here. Figured you'd want an update."

"We were just discussing the loose ends," Tucker said. "What's the latest?"

Reynolds leaned against the wall. "Parsons is talking, trying to get himself a deal. He's confirmed everything Tanya told us. The operation has been running for about fifteen years. They've been moving weapons through from the south to northeastern markets, using Duckwood as a transit hub because of its isolated location and Winson's protection."

"And the murders?" Mallory asked.

"All connected, just as you suspected. Terry Fisher was inducted into the operation by Pastor Pearcy. Apparently, he was a low man on the totem pole; one of the worker bees, if you like. His mistake was he wanted out. He wanted to get married, to start over. Well, they couldn't have that. They couldn't trust him to keep his mouth shut, so they eliminated him."

Tucker nodded. "We figured it must have been something like that. It's a story as old as time. What about the others?"

"Absolutely," Reynolds confirmed. "Cory Robar worked the farm for Parsons occasionally. He stumbled onto something he shouldn't have seen in one of the outbuildings. Malik Williams overheard a conversation between Parsons and Winson. Samuel Jenkins was a county inspector who got suspicious about activity at the farm and began poking around. They caught him nosing around the outbuildings one night. Freddy Paul was actually part of the operation but was skimming profits."

"Has Pearcy been found yet?" Mallory asked.

Reynolds shook his head. "Not yet. But we have officers at

the church and his residence, but, as yet, there's no sign of him. We've issued a BOLO and alerted border patrol in case he tries to leave the country."

"And Louis Fisher?" Tucker prompted. "He was friendly with Tanya, according to the waitress at the café. Did Parsons mention him? Was he involved?"

"Not that I know of," Reynolds said, looking curious. "You think he's connected?"

"I don't know," Tucker admitted. "But he married Terry's fiancée shortly after the murder, and he lied to us about his relationship with Tanya. Those aren't necessarily criminal acts, but they're an anomaly and worth looking into."

"I've got officers going through Tanya's evidence now. If Louis Fisher is involved, there might be something there." Reynolds checked his watch. "Speaking of Tanya, she's being released today. She's agreed to enter witness protection until after the trials."

"She'll need it," Mallory observed. "Pearcy is still out there, and an operation this size probably has connections beyond Duckwood."

"That's exactly why I've got a protective detail with her," Reynolds confirmed. "Now, about you two..." he paused for a moment, then continued, "my department owes you a debt of gratitude. This case might never have been solved, or even come to light, without your persistence."

Tucker shrugged, uncomfortable with praise. "We were just doing our job."

"Still, it's impressive work. I've spoken with your former colleagues at the FBI, by the way. They remember you well."

Tucker tensed slightly. "You contacted the Bureau?"

"Standard procedure with weapons trafficking cases this size. They're sending agents to coordinate the broader investigation, follow the supply chain, identify buyers. Agent Lewis sends his regards, by the way."

Tucker bit his lip. David Lewis, his former supervisor, the man whose bad call had resulted in Marsha Cline's death, the incident that had prompted Tucker's resignation from the FBI.

"Tucker?" Mallory asked, noticing his reaction.

"I'm good," he said, his tone clipped. "When are the FBI agents arriving?"

"They're already here," Reynolds replied, studying Tucker with interest. "Is there something I should know?"

"No," Tucker said firmly. "Ancient history. Water under the bridge. Is there anything else we can help with?"

Reynolds seemed to sense the change in mood. "Not at the moment. Your statements have been processed. You're free to leave when the doctor clears you."

"The doctor already has," Tucker lied smoothly. "We were just about to leave."

After Reynolds left, Mallory turned to him. "Lewis," she said. "It's been a while since we last saw him."

"Not long enough," Tucker said.

"I thought you two had made up," she said.

"We did, sort of, but..." he paused, staring at the floor, then looked up and said, "Let's focus on what's in front of us. I want to talk to Louis Fisher before we leave town."

"Are you sure that's a good idea? You're injured, and if Louis is involved—"

"If he's involved, we need to know," Tucker interrupted. "And I doubt he'd try anything with the town swarming with state police and FBI."

Mallory didn't look convinced, but she knew better than to argue when Tucker used that tone. "Fine. But we go together, and we keep Reynolds informed of our movements."

They checked out of the hospital and retrieved their SUV,

which had been towed to a local garage and hastily repaired after the highway confrontation. The damage was still visible—a cracked windshield, dented rear bumper, and bullet holes in the driver's side door—but it was drivable.

Duckwood looked different in the harsh light of day, its picturesque small-town facade now seeming like a thin veneer over deeper corruption. Police vehicles were stationed throughout the town, and news vans clustered near the municipal building. Locals gathered in small groups, talking in hushed tones about the shocking revelations.

They drove to the hardware store first, but were told Louis Fisher hadn't shown up for work. That in itself was unusual, according to his boss. Louis had never missed a day without calling in.

"Let's try his house," Tucker suggested. "If he's involved, he might be planning to run."

As they approached the Fisher residence, Tucker noticed something wrong immediately. The front door stood partially open, and there was no sign of the family SUV in the driveway.

"Stay behind me," he instructed Mallory, drawing his weapon despite his injured arm. They approached cautiously, Tucker leading the way to the open door.

"Mr. Fisher?" he called out. "Louis Fisher? It's Tucker Randall and Mallory Carver."

No response.

Tucker pushed the door open wider with his foot, revealing a scene of hasty departure. Drawers hung open, contents half-emptied. A suitcase lay on the living room floor, partially packed with children's clothing.

"They left in a hurry," Mallory observed, checking the kitchen. "Recently, too. The coffee pot is still warm."

Tucker moved deeper into the house, checking rooms

systematically. The master bedroom also showed signs of rapid packing—closet doors open, dresser drawers pulled out.

"Tucker," Mallory called from another room. "You need to see this."

He found her in what appeared to be a home office, kneeling beside a small safe that had been left open and emptied. Papers were scattered across the floor, and the desk drawers had been ransacked.

"Someone left in a panic," Tucker observed, scanning the room. "Question is, was it Louis or someone else?"

Mallory held up a document. "It's a deed to property in Mexico. Purchased six months ago in the name of Louis and Tiffany Fisher."

"An escape plan," Tucker said grimly. "Or at least a contingency. But... why would he have left the deed? That makes no sense."

"Maybe it wasn't him," Mallory said. "I mean, it looks to me like someone was looking for something. Maybe Louis disturbed them"

"Anything's possible, I suppose," Tucker said as he moved to the desk, examining the papers strewn across it. Most were ordinary household documents—bills, insurance papers, tax forms. But underneath a scattered pile, he found something more interesting, a photograph of Louis Fisher with Pastor Henry Pearcy, both men in hunting gear, standing over a dead deer. They were smiling broadly, arms around each other's shoulders.

"It appears Louis and Pearcy were friends," he said, holding up the photo for her to see.

She nodded, "They're certainly closer than Louis let on," she replied. "He said Pearcy was just their pastor and performed their wedding. Maybe they're just hunting buddies," she suggested. "That photo doesn't prove criminal involvement."

"No, but it's another connection." Tucker continued searching, finding a bank statement showing regular monthly deposits of $5,000 in cash, far more than a hardware store employee could legitimately earn.

Tucker shook his head. "I think this proves he was involved in something," he said. "I mean, it makes sense that if his cousin Terry was involved, then it's likely he was involved, too."

Mallory didn't answer.

They searched the rest of the house, finding more evidence of a hasty departure, but nothing directly linking Louis to the gunrunning operation. When they returned to the living room, Mallory paused by a family photo on the wall.

"What about Tiffany?" she asked. "Do you think she knew?"

"Hard to say," Tucker replied. "She seemed genuinely distraught about Terry's death, but that doesn't mean she didn't know what Louis was involved in later."

A car pulled into the driveway, and Tucker moved quickly to a window, peering out cautiously. "It's the state police," he said, recognizing Captain Reynolds stepping out of an unmarked vehicle.

Reynolds approached the house, his expression grim. "Thought I might find you here. You should have told me you were visiting a potential suspect."

"We were just following a lead," Tucker explained. "The house was open when we arrived. Looks like the family left in a hurry."

Reynolds surveyed the scene. "We've got a situation developing. Pastor Pearcy has been spotted at a storage facility on the edge of town. Officers attempted to approach him, but he fled inside a unit. He's believed to be armed."

"Is a tactical team on the way?" Tucker asked.

"En route, but it'll take time. The facility is being evacuated now." Reynolds hesitated. "There's more. We found evidence in Tanya's documents that Louis Fisher was not just connected to the gunrunning operation; he was Pearcy's right-hand man. He managed the finances, laundering the money through various off-shore accounts and shell companies."

"Including the hardware store?" Mallory asked.

Reynolds nodded. "And his wife's interior design business. It explains how a hardware store clerk and a part-time designer could afford this house."

"Do you have any idea where they might have gone?" Tucker asked.

Reynolds shook his head. "Nope, but we've put out alerts at airports, bus terminals, and border crossings. But they had at least a few hours' head start." Reynolds glanced around the house again. "Find anything useful here?"

Tucker handed him the property deed and bank statements. "Looks like they may be heading to Mexico. They own property there."

Reynolds nodded. "I'll have our people look into it. Meanwhile, I need to get to that storage facility. According to the officers who spotted him, Pearcy's becoming increasingly unstable. He was talking to himself, behaving erratically."

"We'll come with you," Tucker said immediately.

"With all due respect, you're injured, and this is now a law enforcement operation," Reynolds countered. "You've done more than enough already."

"Captain," Mallory interjected, "we've been investigating these people for days. We might see something your officers would miss. And if Pearcy is unstable, having familiar faces around might help de-escalate the situation."

Reynolds considered this. "You can observe from a safe distance. But I want your word you won't engage unless explicitly authorized."

"Agreed," Tucker said, though he had no intention of standing by if the situation turned dangerous. "Let's go."

18

THEY FOLLOWED REYNOLDS TO THE STORAGE FACILITY—A MODERN complex of ten single-story buildings, each divided into thirty individual units with roll-up doors. A perimeter had already been established, with officers positioned behind vehicles and concrete barriers. The facility manager had provided a diagram showing that Pastor Pearcy was holed up in unit 60, a large corner unit with no windows or alternate exits.

"What's his mental state?" Tucker asked as they joined the command post behind a police SUV.

"Deteriorating," an officer replied, handing Reynolds a radio. "He's been shouting biblical references, claiming he's being persecuted. He says he won't be taken alive."

"Has he made any specific threats?" Mallory asked.

"Nothing beyond refusing to surrender. But the manager confirms he rented the unit six years ago and visits regularly. No one knows what's inside."

"Given what we've learned about the operation, it could be weapons," Reynolds speculated. "Maybe documentation they couldn't risk keeping at the church. A negotiator has been trying to establish communication, but Pearcy's not responding consistently. Now and then, he can be heard reciting scripture or making ominous declarations about judgment day, but so far, he's refused to engage in an actual dialogue."

"SWAT team is ten minutes out," an officer reported. "And FBI agents are also en route."

Tucker tensed at the mention of the FBI, wondering if Lewis would be among them. It was true. They'd put the past behind them more than a year ago, but he'd still not gotten over Marsha Cline's untimely death. *But, it is what it is,* he thought.

"Let me try talking to him," he suggested to Reynolds. "I've interviewed him before. He might respond to a familiar voice."

Reynolds looked skeptical. "He knows you're investigating him. That might make him more volatile, not less."

"True, but he also knows me as someone who listened to him, who treated him with respect. Right now, he's surrounded by anonymous officers with guns. A known face might help."

After considering the options, Reynolds reluctantly agreed. "You can use the bullhorn, but stay behind cover. If he becomes more agitated, we pull back immediately."

Tucker positioned himself behind a concrete barrier, where he could see the door to unit 60 but remain protected. Through the bullhorn, he called out: "Pastor Pearcy. It's Tucker Randall. We spoke at your church yesterday, remember? I'd like to talk to you. Can we do that?"

For a long moment, there was silence. Then the door rattled slightly, and Pearcy's voice came through, strained and higher-pitched than Tucker remembered.

"Mr. Randall? Have you come to witness the final reckoning?"

"No, sir! I've come to talk," Tucker replied evenly. "To understand."

"Understanding comes too late," Pearcy responded, his voice taking on a preacher's cadence. "The wages of sin is death, but the gift of God is eternal life through Jesus Christ our Lord. Romans 6:23."

Tucker glanced at Mallory, who had moved to his side despite his gesture to stay back. "He's quoting scripture about consequences and redemption," she whispered. "Maybe appeal to that?"

"Pastor," Tucker called, "whatever has happened in the past, there's still a chance for truth. For redemption."

A harsh laugh echoed from the storage unit. "Truth? The truth is that I did God's work! Those men were sinners, obstacles to a greater purpose. I simply removed those obstacles. The weapons we moved saved Christian lives in regions where believers are persecuted. The end justified the means!"

Tucker motioned for Mallory to take notes. Pearcy was confessing, and they needed to document it. "Five men died, Pastor. Terry, Cory, Samuel, Malik, Freddy. How was killing them God's work?"

"They were going to destroy everything! Years of mission work, millions in funding for our brothers and sisters abroad." Pearcy's voice grew more agitated. "Terry was the first. He wanted to leave. He would have gone to the authorities. He didn't understand the greater good!"

"And the others?" Tucker prompted, keeping his tone conversational, non-judgmental.

"All the same!" he replied. "They all transgressed. I tried to guide them, to make them understand, but they were blind!"

Reynolds had moved closer, listening intently. "Keep him talking," he whispered. "SWAT's two minutes out."

"Pastor," Tucker continued, "were you alone in this work, or did others help you?"

"There are many servants in the Lord's vineyard," Pearcy replied cryptically. "Winson protected our mission. Parsons provided the means. Louis managed our finances. We were all serving a higher purpose!"

"And Tiffany?" Mallory suddenly called out, ignoring Tucker's warning glance. "Did she know what happened to Terry? That her new husband helped kill her fiancé?"

The question hung in the air for a long, tense moment. Then Pearcy let out a sound that was half laugh, half sob.

"Poor Tiffany. She never knew. Louis made sure of that. She was his prize for faithful service. I blessed their union, though it was built on blood."

Tucker shot Mallory a look—both impressed by her insight and concerned about provoking Pearcy further. But the pastor continued unprompted, his voice growing more unhinged.

"It's all falling apart now. The temple veil is torn asunder. But they won't take me. I've long prepared for this day."

The hairs on the back of Tucker's neck stood up at those words. He turned to Reynolds. "He's going to blow it up. We need to pull back. Now."

But before they could move, a gunshot echoed from inside the storage unit, followed by silence.

"Pastor Pearcy?" Tucker called. No response.

Reynolds motioned for officers to approach cautiously. "Pastor Pearcy, this is the State Police. We're coming in."

Still no response.

The tactical team, which had just arrived, moved into position. On Reynolds' signal, they breached the door of unit 60, rushing inside with weapons raised.

Moments later, an officer emerged and signaled the all-clear. "He's down. Self-inflicted gunshot wound."

Tucker felt a complex mix of emotions: relief that no officers had been harmed, frustration at the loss of a key witness, and a grim satisfaction that Pearcy had at least confessed before taking his own life.

Reynolds approached, his expression somber. "You got him to confess on record. That will help with prosecuting the others."

"What's in the storage unit?" Mallory asked.

"Documents. Lots of them. Financial records, shipping manifests, photographs. And weapons—enough for a small army. This place was essentially their archive and emergency cache."

As crime scene technicians arrived to process the scene, Tucker and Mallory stepped back, watching the activity from a distance.

"It's really over," Mallory said quietly. "Parsons, Winson, and Pearcy are all accounted for. Louis and Tiffany will be found eventually."

Tucker nodded, but his expression remained troubled. "There's still something I want to understand. Why did Tanya date both Terry and Malik? Was it just coincidence, or was she somehow involved?"

"We can ask her," Mallory suggested. "She's still at the hospital."

But before they could leave, a black SUV pulled up, and three people in suits emerged. Tucker recognized one of them immediately; David Lewis, his former FBI supervisor, looking older but still carrying himself with the same officious authority that had grated on Tucker all those years ago.

"Tucker. Mallory," Lewis said, approaching with an extended hand. "It's been a while, but it's good to see you both again. It's not something I expected, and definitely not on a case like this."

Tucker shook his hand briefly, his expression neutral. "Agent Lewis. You're heading the Bureau's involvement?"

"Coordinating with state and local authorities, yes." Lewis glanced at the storage facility. "I understand the pastor took the easy way out."

"After confessing to orchestrating five murders," Tucker replied evenly.

Lewis nodded. "Good work on that. The Bureau's been tracking weapons movements through this corridor for years, but we never connected it to Duckwood. Sometimes it takes local knowledge to break these cases."

There was something in the way he said it, a hint of condescension that he regarded Tucker's career change from FBI agent to private investigator as a step down.

"It's good to see you, too, David, but..." he glanced at Mallory, then continued, "We should be going. We still have loose ends to tie up."

"Actually," Lewis said, "I'd appreciate it if you'd stick around. Your insights could be valuable to our investigation, especially given your history with this case."

Tucker caught the subtle emphasis on the word "history." Was it a subtle reminder of the Marsha Cline case, of Tucker's resignation, of the bad blood between them?

"We've provided statements to Captain Reynolds," Tucker replied. "Everything we know is in the reports."

David smiled thinly. "Of course. Well, if you remember anything else, you know how to reach me."

As they walked to their SUV, Mallory glanced back at Lewis. "He seems nice enough," she said. "A bit of an improvement since the last time we saw him."

Tucker nodded once, his jaw tight. "He'll never change. Let's go see Tanya. I want to wrap this up and get back to Chattanooga."

They drove to the hospital in silence, Tucker lost in memories he'd rather forget, Mallory respecting his need for space. The case was essentially solved, the conspiracy exposed, but personal ghosts were harder to lay to rest than the cold case murders.

19

MALLORY WATCHED TUCKER AS THEY MADE THEIR WAY THROUGH the hospital corridors toward Tanya Broadbent's room. His encounter with former FBI supervisor David Lewis had left him tense, his jaw set in the way she recognized as his defense mechanism against unwelcome emotions. She knew better than to press him about it, and that Tucker would talk when he was ready to, or more likely, he wouldn't talk about it at all.

Two state police officers stood outside Tanya's room, confirming Reynolds' promise of protection. They nodded at Tucker and Mallory, recognizing them from the events at the Parsons farm.

"Ms. Broadbent's awake," one of the officers informed them. "Captain Reynolds said you might be stopping by. You can go on in."

"Thanks," Tucker said with a nod of his head, then grabbed the door handle, pushed the door open, and stepped inside.

Tanya was sitting up in bed, looking much better than when they'd last seen her being rushed away from the farmhouse. The bruises on her face had darkened, but her eyes were clear and alert. She was wearing a hospital gown and had an IV in one arm, but otherwise appeared ready to leave.

"Hah! The investigators," she said by way of greeting. "I was wondering if you'd come back."

"We have a few more questions," Tucker replied, pulling up a chair. "If you're feeling up to it."

Tanya gestured to the TV mounted on the wall, which was showing news coverage of the raid on the Parsons farm. "I've been watching. Quite the show you two kicked off."

"It hardly begins to cover it," Mallory said, taking the other chair. "Tanya, we need to understand your role in all this. Specifically, your relationships with Terry Fisher and Malik Williams."

Tanya's expression sobered. "I wondered when you'd ask about that." She sighed, adjusting her position in the bed. "I dated Terry briefly in high school. Nothing serious, just teenage stuff. We stayed friends afterward, even when he got together with Tiffany."

"And Malik?" Tucker prompted.

"That was years later. I'd been away from Duckwood for a while, living in Memphis, trying to escape this place." A shadow crossed her face. "Malik was from here, but I met him there. We dated for about a year before he got a job offer back here in Duckwood. I came back with him, thinking maybe the town had changed."

"But it hadn't," Mallory guessed.

"No. It was the same old Duckwood, just with different paint." Tanya ran a hand through her tangled hair. "Malik was working construction. Good money, steady work. Then one day, he overheard Parsons and the pastor talking about a shipment. He didn't know what it meant at first, but he mentioned it to me."

"And you recognized it as suspicious because of what happened to Terry," Tucker said, watching her closely.

Tanya nodded. "Terry had told me things, back when we were friends. Not much, really. Just that he'd gotten himself into a mess and wanted out, and that he was going to talk to Pastor Pearcy about it."

"But instead, Pearcy turned him over to Parsons," Mallory said.

"I sort of figured that out later, after Terry was killed. But from what I've learned since, I think it was Pearcy that killed him, not Parsons. At the time, it just seemed like a random tragedy. But when Malik mentioned the conversation he'd overheard..." Tanya's voice tightened. "I warned him to keep his mouth shut. I was afraid. But Malik was a righteous man. He thought he should report it to the police."

"To Winson," Tucker said.

"Yes. And he did, and three days later, Malik was dead. Same as Terry—two shots to the back of the head." Tanya's eyes glistened with tears she refused to let fall. "That's when I knew for sure. They were killing anyone who threatened to expose them."

"So you started collecting evidence," Mallory said.

Tanya nodded. "I did! Carefully. Slowly. I knew if they suspected me, I'd be next. So I got a job at the café. It was a good place to overhear things. I pretended to be a burnout that nobody needed to worry about."

"And Louis Fisher?" Tucker asked. "The waitress said you two were friendly."

A brittle laugh escaped Tanya. "Louis thought he was recruiting me. After Malik died, Louis approached me, acting sympathetic. Said he could get me 'work' if I needed money. Small jobs at first delivering packages, picking up cash. I played along, documenting everything."

"You were building a case," Mallory said, impressed by Tanya's courage and persistence.

"I was getting justice for Malik. And Terry. And the others."

Tanya's expression hardened. "For a while, Louis thought I was just another useful idiot. Then he started trusting me with more information, thinking I was fully on board."

"How deeply was Louis involved?" Tucker asked.

"He was essential," Tanya replied without hesitation. "He was the money man. Parsons and Pearcy handled the hardware operations and connections, but Louis managed the finances. He set up shell companies, laundered the profits through legitimate businesses. He was good with numbers, and nobody suspected the quiet guy at the hardware store."

"And Tiffany?" Mallory asked, remembering Pearcy's words at the storage unit. "Did she know?"

Tanya shook her head. "I don't think she did. I think Louis kept her in the dark. She was his respectability, his cover, the grieving fiancée who found comfort with her dead boyfriend's cousin. Who would question that story?"

Mallory exchanged a glance with Tucker. They'd both wondered about Tiffany's involvement, given her quick relationship with Louis after Terry's murder.

"What was in the evidence you collected?" Tucker inquired. "Reynolds mentioned documents, but he wasn't specific."

"Everything," Tanya said with a hint of pride. "Photos of meetings between Parsons, Pearcy, and the buyers. Financial records Louis didn't know I'd photographed. Names, dates, locations of shipments. Recordings of conversations for years I'd gathered bit by bit."

"That was a dangerous game you were playing," Mallory observed. "What made you decide to use it now?"

Tanya's expression darkened. "I overheard Parsons and Pearcy discussing a major expansion. They were bringing in partners from out of state, planning to increase shipments through Duckwood. More guns, more money... and inevitably, more deaths to keep it quiet. I couldn't let that happen."

"So you were going to expose them?" Tucker asked.

"I'd arranged to meet a journalist from Nashville on Tuesday," Tanya confirmed. "But they found out somehow. Monday night, after my shift at the café, Parsons and his son were waiting at my house."

She described her captivity briefly, how they'd questioned her about the evidence, moved her from location to location as they searched her home, and finally brought her to the shed when Tucker and Mallory appeared and the state police began closing in.

"So, what happens now?" she asked when she'd finished. "Reynolds mentioned witness protection."

"It's the safest option," Tucker said. "The operation may have been centered in Duckwood, but there are likely connections to larger criminal organizations. People who might want to silence you."

"Plus, Louis and Tiffany are still out there," Mallory added. "They fled before the raid."

Tanya nodded, "I'm not surprised," she said. "Louis always had contingency plans. He called it his 'insurance policy.' I think he bought some property somewhere, and I know he had cash reserves."

"He has property in Mexico," Tucker said. "We found a deed at their house."

"That makes sense. Louis spoke Spanish, and he had connections south of the border; his weapons source." Tanya sighed. "So I just... disappear then? New name, new life, all that stuff you see on TV?"

"Until the trials are over, at least," Mallory said gently. "It's the only way to ensure your safety."

A knock at the door interrupted them. A nurse entered, followed by a state police officer Mallory didn't recognize.

"Ms. Broadbent needs rest," the nurse announced firmly.

"And her transport team has arrived."

The officer nodded to Tucker and Mallory. "We're moving her to a secure location for witness protection processing. Captain Reynolds sent me to let you know."

Tucker nodded, then turned away and called Reynolds. "I have an officer here— Okay. That's all I wanted to know." He ended the call, turned to Mallory and Tanya and nodded. The officer smiled knowingly at him.

They stood to leave, but Tanya reached out, catching Mallory's hand. "Thank you," she said quietly. "For believing me. For stopping them."

"You did most of the work," Mallory replied with a smile. "We just helped finish it."

Outside in the corridor, Tucker checked his watch. "It's getting late. We should head back to the hotel, pack up, and leave for Chattanooga in the morning."

Mallory nodded, suddenly realizing how exhausted she was. The adrenaline of the past few days was wearing off, leaving her drained. "Food first? I'm starving."

They found a quiet diner away from the center of Duckwood, where they'd be less likely to encounter curious locals or news reporters. Over burgers and fries, they discussed what they'd learned from Tanya, filling in the final pieces of the conspiracy.

"It's impressive," Mallory said, stirring her milkshake with a straw. "What Tanya accomplished. Working alone for years, gathering evidence, risking her life."

"She was driven by personal loss," Tucker observed. "Sometimes that's the most powerful motivation."

"Like Gary Fisher," Mallory agreed. "Eleven years, and he never gave up on finding justice for his brother."

Tucker nodded, his expression distant. "I should call him, let him know what we've learned about Terry's murder. The official investigation will take time to process all the evidence."

"I'm sure he's been following the news coverage," Mallory said. "But yes, he deserves to hear it from us directly."

As they finished their meal, Mallory's phone rang. It was Jen, calling for the third time that day. With a grimace, Mallory answered.

"Before you ask, yes, I'm alive," she said.

"I can see that on the news!" Jen's voice was a mixture of relief and exasperation. "You and Tucker are all over every channel! 'Private investigators crack decade-old murder conspiracy.' Mom and Dad have been calling non-stop."

"Sorry," Mallory said, genuinely contrite. "Things happened quickly. We uncovered a gunrunning operation, and—"

"I know! It's all the reporters are talking about." Jen's tone softened. "Are you okay? I mean really okay?"

"We're fine. Tucker got a minor gunshot wound, but—"

"A gunshot wound? Oh...m'God!" Jen's voice rose sharply.

"It's just a graze," Mallory assured her, catching Tucker's amused glance across the table. "Just a few stitches. He's already out of the hospital. We're heading back to Chattanooga tomorrow."

"Thank God. Does that mean you'll make the dress appointment?"

Mallory had completely forgotten about the wedding plans amid the chaos of the past few days. "Yes, I'll be there. Promise."

After ending the call, she found Tucker watching her with a faint smile. "Wedding planning calls? Even after solving five murders and exposing a weapons trafficking ring?"

"Some things wait for nothing," Mallory replied with a rueful laugh. "Not even near-death experiences."

Back at the hotel, they found a note from Captain Reynolds slipped under their door, updating them on the investigation's progress. The evidence from Pearcy's storage unit had yielded a wealth of information, confirming much of what Tanya had told them. Louis and Tiffany Fisher were still at large, but border patrol had been alerted, and their financial accounts frozen, those they could find.

Tucker made a brief call to Gary Fisher, providing a simplified version of what they'd discovered. From Mallory's side of the conversation, she could tell Gary was emotional but grateful for finally having answers he and his parents needed.

As Tucker hung up, Mallory felt a familiar sense of closure that came with completing a troublesome case. Justice had been served, to the extent it could be for victims long dead. Conspirators had been exposed, an illegal operation dismantled.

"I think we did good, Tucker," she said, sitting on the edge of her bed.

Tucker nodded, checking the bandage on his arm. "And a dangerous operation has been shut down. Who knows how many lives that might save down the line."

"What do you think will happen to Winson and Parsons?" Mallory asked.

"Federal weapons charges, five counts of conspiracy to commit murder, obstruction of justice..." Tucker shrugged. "They'll never see the outside of a prison again."

"And Louis and Tiffany?"

"They'll be found, eventually. People on the run make mistakes, especially with children in tow."

Mallory nodded, considering this. "It's hard to believe Louis was involved in his own cousin's murder. That's... That's family betrayal at its worst."

"According to Pearcy, Louis didn't directly participate in Terry's murder," Tucker pointed out. "But he certainly benefited from it. He got Terry's fiancée, a position in the organization.

And he helped cover it up for years. Say what you want. Louis Fisher is a badass."

"And all the while playing the supportive cousin who stepped in to help the grieving Tiffany." Mallory shook her head in disgust. "Some people can compartmentalize anything."

Tucker was quiet for a moment, his expression distant. "We all have our compartments, Mal. Ways of separating and hiding the parts of ourselves we don't want to face."

Mallory recognized this was as close as Tucker would come to discussing his reaction to seeing David Lewis again, so she decided on a gentle approach. "Tucker, I thought you two made up before he left after we closed out Vinny's case last year."

"We did," Tucker said, "but you know, there are some things you just can't easily dismiss. What he did is one of them. The Marsha Cline case... it's one of those things. She was only nineteen. It should never have happened. David never did take responsibility for it."

"So that's it?" she asked. "You're never going to be able to put it behind you?"

Tucker shrugged, then winced as pain shot through his injured arm. "One day, perhaps. In the meantime, I'll get along with him when I have to. Other than that..." he trailed off.

He fell silent, the memory clearly still painful despite the years that had passed since Marsha's death. Mallory didn't press him further.

"It wasn't your fault, Tucker," she said simply.

"I know that," Tucker replied. "But knowing something and feeling it are two entirely different things."

They lapsed into silence, Mallory respecting Tucker's need for space after sharing even that small piece of his past. Eventually, she stood and gathered her toiletries. "I'm going to shower. Early start tomorrow?"

Tucker nodded, seemingly grateful for the change of subject.

"Yep!" he said, brightly. "Six o'clock. I want to write and deliver our final report for Gary Fisher before we start back to Chattanooga. I'd like to be on the road by eleven. That should get us back in time for lunch. I have a hankering for some decent Mexican."

In the shower, Mallory let the hot water wash away some of the tension and fatigue of the past few days. Her thoughts drifted to the dress appointment, to the wedding plans that had been put on hold during this investigation. The juxtaposition seemed almost surreal. Planning a celebration of life and partnership while dealing with murder and betrayal.

Yet perhaps it was fitting. Their work as investigators was all about seeking justice, restoring order from chaos. Marriage was another kind of order, a commitment to building something positive together despite the darkness they often encountered in their profession.

"Room for one more?" Tucker asked.

"Always," she said and stepped to one side to make room for him.

When she finally emerged from the bathroom, Tucker was sitting on his bed, a towel wrapped around his waist, making notes in his precise handwriting. Always documenting, always ensuring the details were preserved accurately. It was one of the many things she admired about him: his thoroughness, his dedication to getting things right.

"What are you thinking about?" he asked, noticing her thoughtful expression.

"Life. Death. Wedding dresses, moments together in the shower." Mallory smiled. "The usual post-case existential pondering."

Tucker's expression softened slightly. "That dress appointment is important to you and Jen, isn't it? You should definitely make it."

"I will." She sat across from him on her own bed. "And you should definitely have an opinion on what kind of cake we serve. That's your one wedding planning assignment."

"I can handle cake decisions," he agreed with a rare smile. "As long as it's not during an active murder investigation."

"Deal." Mallory yawned, the exhaustion finally catching up with her. "I think I'm going to crash now. Wake me when it's time to leave?"

"Don't I always?" Tucker replied, returning to his notes.

As Mallory drifted toward sleep, images from the past few days flashed through her mind: Terry Fisher's autopsy photos, Tanya's determined face as she escaped her captors, Pastor Pearcy's storage unit filled with weapons and secrets, the fear in Winson's eyes as he realized his crimes had been exposed.

But these were gradually replaced by more pleasant thoughts: Tucker's steady presence throughout the investigation, the satisfaction of bringing closure, the wedding plans waiting for her in Chattanooga, and the beautiful, gentle moment in the shower. And finally, life continuing, as it always did, even after confronting the darkest aspects of human nature.

Tomorrow they would return home, file their reports, and close this chapter. But tonight, she would rest, knowing they had done what they set out to do: uncover the truth about Terry Fisher's murder. She smiled to herself as she drifted away. *And a whole... lot...... more...*

It was at that moment Tucker's phone buzzed, showing an unfamiliar number with a Washington, D.C. area code.

20

"Tucker Randall," he answered cautiously.

"Agent Randall. Or should I say, Mr. Randall now?"

Tucker stiffened, recognizing the voice immediately. "Director Hargrove. It's been a while."

FBI Director Alan Hargrove had been Tucker's ultimate superior during his Bureau days, a man he'd respected but rarely interacted with directly.

"Indeed it has. I've been following your work in Duckwood. It was an impressive investigation."

"Thank you, sir," Tucker replied automatically, years of Bureau protocol kicking in. "But I'm not sure why that would warrant a call from the Director."

"Let's just say I take a personal interest when former agents distinguish themselves, especially in cases involving weapons trafficking across state lines." Hargrove's tone remained pleasant, but carried an underlying significance. "Agent Lewis speaks highly of your work."

Tucker nearly scoffed at that. To his knowledge, Lewis had never spoken highly of him, not even before the Marsha Cline incident. "That's... surprising to hear," he said.

"People change, Randall. Perspectives shift with time." Hargrove paused. "The Bureau is establishing a new task force focused on domestic weapons trafficking. We need experienced people who understand how these operations work. People who can think independently, who aren't afraid to pursue uncomfortable truths."

The implication was clear, and Tucker felt a momentary vertigo, as if the past few years had suddenly collapsed, offering a return to the career path he'd abandoned. "Sir, I appreciate the implied offer, but I'm settled in Chattanooga now. My partner and I have built something here."

"Your fiancée, Ms. Carver, would be an asset to the Bureau as well. Her background and intuition would bring a valuable perspective."

Tucker glanced at Mallory, who was now awake and watching him with a mixture of curiosity and concern, clearly able to hear only his side of the conversation. "That's not a decision I can make unilaterally, sir."

"Of course not," Hargrove agreed. "Just something to consider. The official offer will come through proper channels if you're interested. Take some time, discuss it with Ms. Carver. The task force doesn't begin operations for another month."

After ending the call, Tucker set his phone down carefully, feeling Mallory's questioning gaze.

"The FBI Director?" she asked. "What did he want?"

Tucker summarized the conversation, watching her expression shift from surprise to thoughtfulness. "He's offering us both positions with a new task force, the focus being nationwide weapons trafficking."

"Us?" Mallory repeated. "Both of us? Me, an FBI agent. Come on, Tucker. The FBI doesn't work that way. It's you they want and they're using me as bait."

"I dunno," he replied. "Hargrove doesn't always follow standard protocols." He leaned back in his chair, processing the unexpected development. "It's a significant opportunity."

"But?" Mallory prompted, hearing the reservation in his voice.

"But it would mean returning to a system I deliberately left. Working under superiors like Lewis again, following directives I might not agree with." He met her gaze directly. "And it would probably mean relocating, postponing the wedding, starting over somewhere new."

Mallory considered this. "Would it be worth it? Going back to the Bureau?"

Tucker didn't answer immediately, genuinely uncertain. His departure from the FBI had been a principled stand, a rejection of a system that had prioritized expediency over safety in the Marsha Cline case. But he couldn't deny that the resources and reach of the Bureau far exceeded what they could accomplish as private investigators.

"I don't know," he admitted finally. "It's not a decision we need to make tonight. Or even this week."

"Agreed," Mallory said. "Let's get some rest, and tackle this with clear heads later."

He nodded. "Go back to sleep, Mal. We have an early start tomorrow."

As he watched Mallory close her eyes, he considered the life they'd built together in Chattanooga. Their partnership, both professional and personal, had brought him more satisfaction than his years with the Bureau. They worked well together, balanced each other's strengths and weaknesses, and most importantly, made their own decisions about which cases to take and how to pursue them.

Would returning to the FBI—even with Mallory alongside

him—provide the same fulfillment? Or would the bureaucracy and chain of command eventually become as frustrating as before?

These were the questions that haunted Tucker as he lay down to sleep.

21

It was just after nine the following morning when Tucker loaded their bags into the SUV. The morning air was crisp, carrying the scent of dew-covered grass and distant wood smoke. The town looked peaceful, almost innocent, as if the events of the past few days had been a collective nightmare rather than reality.

He checked his bandaged arm, finding it stiff but manageable. The injury was minor compared to what could have happened if those bullets had found more vital targets. A few inches difference, and Mallory might be driving back to Chattanooga alone.

Speaking of Mallory, she emerged from the hotel with their last bag and a cardboard tray holding two large coffee cups. "Ready to leave this charming town behind?" she asked, handing him a coffee.

"More than ready," Tucker replied, taking a grateful sip. "Though I doubt Duckwood will forget us anytime soon."

That was an understatement. Their investigation had exposed corruption at the highest levels of local authority. The small town would be dealing with the aftermath for years to come.

———

THE FISHER HOME looked different in daylight than it had during their first visit. The morning sun cast a warm glow over the modest house, and the front yard was quiet, the children presumably at school. Tucker pulled into the driveway. "Ready?" he asked Mallory as he tucked the folder containing their final report securely under his arm.

She nodded, staring out through the windshield, noting the subtle signs of a house where there was sickness: a wheelchair ramp recently added to the side entrance, curtains drawn in what was likely the master bedroom, a medical supply company's delivery notice still taped to the door.

They exited the car and walked up onto the front porch. Gary opened the door before they could knock, as if he'd been watching for their arrival. His expression was a mixture of anticipation and trepidation, the look of a man both eager and afraid to hear final confirmation of long-suspected truths.

"Mr. Randall, Ms. Carver. Please, come in. My parents are in the living room."

They followed him through the hallway into a living room transformed into a makeshift bedroom. Bill Fisher sat in a recliner, oxygen tubes in his nostrils, a blanket across his legs despite the warm day. Beside him in a comfortable chair, Margaret Fisher, thin and frail but with alert eyes, assessed the visitors carefully. Remembering the photo in the file, Mallory couldn't help but notice the familial resemblance to Terry visible in both parents: Bill's strong jawline, Margaret's expressive eyes.

"Mom, Dad, these are the investigators I told you about," Gary said, gently.

"Thank you for coming," Bill Fisher said, his voice surprisingly strong despite his obvious physical weakness. "After all these years," he said. "I'd nearly given up hope of knowing the truth."

Tucker approached, shaking the old man's hand gently. His grip was surprisingly strong.

"Mr. Fisher. Mrs. Fisher," he said. "This is my partner, Mallory Carver. We're glad we could provide some answers, sir. We've prepared a complete report of our findings."

He handed the folder to Bill, who took it with trembling hands, but made no move to open it.

"Why don't you tell us in your own words," Margaret suggested, her voice soft but steady. "The report will be there when we're ready."

Tucker nodded, taking a seat across from the elderly couple while Mallory sat nearby.

"Your son Terry was murdered because he wanted to do the right thing. He got in with some bad people, and he wanted out," Tucker said. "He wanted a clean start and to marry Tiffany, and it got him killed. He didn't know what he was getting into, and as soon as he did... Well, he talked to Pastor Pearcy, not realizing the pastor's involvement, and he unknowingly signed his own death warrant."

Bill's hand sought his wife's, gripping it tightly as Tucker continued explaining the conspiracy, how Pearcy, Parsons, Winson and eventually Louis Fisher had operated the gunrunning operation, using Duckwood's isolated location as a transit hub for illegal weapons. He explained how over the years following Terry's death, the other victims had each stumbled upon different aspects of the operation, and how they'd been systematically eliminated to protect the conspiracy.

"So it was our own pastor who pulled the trigger?" Margaret asked, her voice breaking slightly. "The man who conducted Terry's funeral was the one who killed him?"

"Yes," Mallory confirmed gently. "He admitted it just before he killed himself. Not in so many words, but yes, he killed all five victims personally."

"And Louis?" Gary asked, his expression hardened at the mention of his cousin. "Was he involved in Terry's death?"

"According to Pearcy's confession, Louis wasn't directly involved in planning or carrying out Terry's murder," Tucker explained. "But he learned about it afterward and he helped cover it up. Later, he became more deeply involved, managing the financial affairs of the operation."

"And he married Tiffany," Bill said, his voice tight with anger. "My brother's boy married my son's fiancée, knowing all along..."

"The evidence suggests Tiffany didn't know anything about it, that she was kept in the dark," Mallory interjected softly. "She appears to have been an unwitting part of Louis's cover. When the operation was exposed, he fled with her and their children. We heard just before we arrived here that they've since been apprehended trying to cross into Mexico."

A heavy silence fell over the room as the Fisher family absorbed these revelations. Gary stood by the window, his back partly turned as he processed the confirmation of his cousin's betrayal. Bill stared at the folder in his lap, one gnarled finger tracing Terry's name on the cover.

"I knew it had to be something like this," Margaret finally said. "Terry was a good boy. Not perfect, but good-hearted. He wouldn't have been mixed up in anything sordid. I'm so glad you found out he died because he was trying to do the right thing."

"All the evidence points to that conclusion," Tucker agreed.

Bill looked up, his eyes suddenly fierce despite his frail body. "Will they pay for what they did? All of them?"

"Parsons and Winson are in federal custody, facing federal weapons charges and multiple counts of conspiracy to commit murder," Tucker assured him. "Louis will be extradited back to Tennessee and will face similar charges. The evidence against them is overwhelming, particularly with Tanya Broadbent's documentation and Pearcy's confession."

"Tanya," Gary said, turning from the window. "She dated Terry briefly in high school, didn't she?"

Mallory nodded. "And later she dated Malik Williams, another victim. After Malik's murder, she spent years gathering evidence against the conspiracy, putting herself at considerable risk. Her testimony and documentation will be crucial in the prosecutions."

"We owe her a debt," Bill said quietly. "Her and you two. Eleven years we've waited, wondering, imagining the worst."

"Knowing is better," Margaret added, reaching for the folder. "Even the painful truth is better than the endless uncertainty."

She opened the report, and she and Bill leaned together as they began to read the detailed account of their son's final days. Gary stepped closer to Tucker and Mallory, gesturing toward the kitchen.

"Let's give them some privacy," he suggested, leading the investigators to the adjoining room.

In the kitchen, Gary poured coffee into three mugs with mechanical precision, his movements suggesting a man on autopilot. "I should feel relief," he said finally. "After all this time, knowing what happened, why it happened."

"But?" Mallory prompted gently.

"But I don't. I just feel... hollow." Gary passed them the mugs. "All these years searching for the truth, and now that I have it, nothing's changed. Terry's still gone. My parents are still dying. Louis, who I grew up with, who I trusted, still betrayed our family in the worst possible way."

"Closure isn't the same as healing," Tucker observed quietly. "One is knowing what happened. The other is learning to live with that knowledge."

Gary nodded slowly. "That makes sense. I suppose the healing part comes next, now that we have the closure."

"Your parents seem like strong people," Mallory said. "And so do you. You didn't give up on finding justice for Terry, even when it would have been easier to let it go."

"I couldn't let it go," Gary admitted. "Not while my parents were still alive, still hoping for answers. Now at least they can..." His voice caught, and he took a moment to compose himself. "At least they can go with that burden lifted."

They spoke a while longer, Gary asking detailed questions about the investigation that hadn't been covered in their brief phone conversations. Tucker answered each query patiently, providing as much clarity as possible without being unnecessarily graphic about Terry's final moments.

When they returned to the living room, Bill had the report open in his lap, but his eyes were closed, oxygen hissing softly through his tubes. Margaret looked up as they entered.

"He got tired," she explained softly. "But he read enough. We both did." Her gaze shifted to Tucker and Mallory. "Thank you for not giving up on our boy. For making sure those responsible will face justice."

"It was our privilege," Mallory replied sincerely.

As they prepared to leave, Margaret reached for Mallory's hand. "Terry would have been about your age now. Maybe married, with children of his own." Her eyes glistened with unshed tears. "I hope you two have a long, happy life together. Not everyone gets that chance."

The comment caught Mallory off guard. They hadn't

mentioned their engagement to the Fisher family. Margaret smiled at her surprise.

"I notice things," she said simply. "The way you work together, the ring on your finger. Life is precious. Don't waste a moment of it."

Tucker nodded, looked at Mallory and said, "Time to go, I think."

She nodded. They said their goodbyes and, with more than a little reluctance, they left the Fisher family to their thoughts.

22

AS THEY PULLED AWAY FROM THE FISHER HOME, TUCKER DROVE slowly along the main street, noticing how empty it seemed compared to when they'd arrived. State police vehicles were still visible near the municipal building, and a few news vans remained parked nearby, but the usual morning bustle of a small town was notably absent.

"It's like a ghost town," Mallory observed, echoing his thoughts.

"People are staying home, processing what happened. Finding out your police chief and pastor were criminal conspirators isn't an everyday occurrence."

Mallory sighed. "This place will never be the same."

"Yes, it will," Tucker said as he steered the SUV toward the highway that would take them back to Chattanooga. "Time is a great healer. They'll get over it."

They fell into a comfortable silence as they left Duckwood behind, both lost in their own thoughts. Tucker reviewed the case mentally, a habit from his FBI days, analyzing what they'd done right, what they could have done better, what lessons they could apply to future investigations.

They'd accomplished their primary objective: discovering who killed Terry Fisher and why and, in the process, they'd uncovered a conspiracy far larger than they'd initially suspected and provided closure for four other families as well.

"You know, I've been thinking about Detective Bradley," Mallory said suddenly, interrupting his thoughts. "How he tried to investigate the gunrunning angle eleven years ago and was shut down. I hope he finds some peace knowing he was right all along."

"We should visit him again before we leave the area," Tucker suggested. "Let him know how it all turned out. It shouldn't take but ten minutes, or so."

Mallory checked her watch. "The nursing home should be open for visitors by the time we get there. It's on our way back to Chattanooga, anyway."

Tucker adjusted their route, taking the exit that would lead them to the Golden Years Retirement Home. Thirty minutes later, they pulled into the facility's parking lot, noting how peaceful it seemed compared to the chaos they'd left behind.

Inside, the receptionist recognized them from their previous visit. "You're here to see Mr. Bradley? He's having a good morning today. He actually mentioned that he hoped you might come back."

They found the retired detective in the same sunroom where they'd first interviewed him, but his appearance had changed subtly. He sat straighter in his wheelchair, his eyes clearer, as if a burden had been lifted from his shoulders.

"The dynamic duo returns," he greeted them with a small smile. "I've been watching the news. That's quite the hornet's nest you two stirred up."

"We thought you'd want to know how it ended," Tucker said, taking a seat across from him.

"Oh, I already know that," he said, perkily. "It's all anyone here has been talking about. Duckwood's biggest scandal in living memory." Bradley's expression grew more serious. "You confirmed what I suspected all those years ago. The gunrunning, Parsons' involvement, Winson looking the other way."

"You were right about everything," Mallory assured him. "Your initial investigation was on the right track. They derailed it deliberately."

"My 'accident,'" Bradley nodded. "Not so accidental after all, I'm guessing."

"Probably not," Tucker acknowledged. "Pearcy confessed before he died that they eliminated anyone who threatened to expose them."

"Pearcy." Bradley shook his head slowly. "I never would have suspected the pastor, even though the first body was found on his leased land. He hid behind that collar very effectively."

Tucker updated Bradley on the details they'd learned—how the operation worked, Louis Fisher's role in managing the finances, Tanya's years-long evidence gathering, the arrests, and Pearcy's suicide.

"You've given an old man some peace," Bradley said when Tucker finished. "I've spent eleven years wondering if I missed something, if I could have done more for those families."

"You did everything you could," Mallory assured him. "Against powerful people who were determined to stop you."

They spent another twenty minutes with Bradley, answering his questions about the investigation. Tucker was impressed by the old detective's sharp memory and insightful observations, despite his advancing age and health issues. The man had been a good investigator, stymied not by lack of skill but by corruption beyond his control.

As they prepared to leave, Bradley reached out, gripping Tucker's hand with surprising strength. "One piece of advice from someone who's been where you are. Don't let the job consume you." His gaze shifted meaningfully to Mallory. "There's more to life than catching the bad guys. Took me too long to learn that."

Tucker nodded, understanding the message. "We're working on that balance," he said, glancing at Mallory. "In fact, we're heading back to Chattanooga for a wedding dress appointment."

Bradley smiled. "Good. Hold on to that. The cases will always be there, but the people we care about won't."

Back in the car, Mallory gave Tucker a curious look. "Wedding dress appointment, huh? I didn't think you were keeping track of that schedule."

"Jen's called you three times about it," he replied. "It would be hard to miss," Tucker started the engine. "Besides, you deserve to focus on something positive after all that's happened."

"We both do," Mallory said, settling into her seat. "Maybe you could actually come to the appointment with me, give an opinion."

Tucker's expression must have betrayed his horror at the suggestion, because Mallory laughed. "I'm kidding. I know that's beyond your comfort zone. Focus on the cake decision like we agreed."

On the drive back to Chattanooga, Tucker was quieter than usual, his expression thoughtful.

"What's on your mind?" Mallory finally asked as the city skyline came into view.

"Margaret Fisher," he replied. "What she said about not wasting time. About Terry never getting the chance to build a life with someone he loved."

"It got to me too," Mallory admitted.

"Our work reminds us constantly of how fragile life is," Tucker continued. "How quickly it can be taken away. Maybe that's why I've been reconsidering Hargrove's offer after all."

"Oh, you have, have you?" she said, slightly concerned. "And?"

"Life is too short to make decisions based on old grudges or fears. If working with the Bureau in some capacity allows us to make a larger impact while still maintaining what matters to us..." He glanced at her briefly. "Well, maybe it's worth considering, don't you think?"

Mallory nodded, understanding what this admission cost him. For Tucker to even contemplate returning to the organization he'd left on principle showed significant personal change.

"We'll figure it out," she assured him. "Together. That's what partnerships are all about."

As they reached the city limits, Mallory felt a sense of one chapter closing and another beginning. The Fisher family had their answers after eleven years of uncertainty. Now it was time for her and Tucker to determine their own next steps, as private investigators and partners in every sense of the word, or to become part of something bigger, much bigger.

The drive to Chattanooga had taken just under ninety minutes, the familiar skyline welcoming them back to normal life, or as normal as life ever got in their profession. Tucker drove directly to his home office to find it exactly as they'd left it four days earlier, though it felt like months had passed.

"We should call it a day," Mallory suggested, noticing the time. "Finish the report tomorrow. I'm exhausted, and you need rest with that arm."

Tucker was about to protest, but then decided she was right. Some decisions couldn't be rushed, especially those that would affect not just his future, but Mallory's as well.

23

MALLORY SMOOTHED DOWN THE SATIN OF THE FIFTH DRESS SHE'D tried on, studying her reflection in the three-way mirror. Bridal Elegance was everything the name suggested—elegant, upscale, and filled with more wedding dresses than she'd ever seen in one place. Jen sat on a plush velvet chair nearby, watching with a critical eye as Mallory turned slowly.

"That's the one," Jen declared, her expression softening. "You look beautiful, Mal."

Mallory had to admit; the dress was perfect. The A-line silhouette complemented her figure. The sweetheart neckline was flattering without being too revealing, and the delicate lace overlay added just enough detail without overwhelming her frame. Most importantly, she could imagine moving comfortably in it during an outdoor ceremony.

"It feels right," she agreed, swishing the skirt gently. "Not too formal for the botanical garden, but still special."

The bridal consultant beamed. "We can add a simple belt with a bit of sparkle to accentuate your waist. And a chapel-length veil would complement the train beautifully."

Jen stood, circling Mallory with a practiced eye. "She's right.

A bit of sparkle at the waist would be perfect. What do you think?"

For a moment, Mallory's mind flashed to the events of the past week—crouching behind a tractor in a dark barn, fleeing armed men on a rural highway, watching Pastor Pearcy's psychological breakdown. The contrast between that reality and this moment of traditional feminine ritual was almost disorienting.

"Mal?" Jen prompted, noticing her distraction. "The belt?"

"Yes, let's see it," Mallory agreed, pulling her focus back to the present. This was important too, a different kind of important than solving murders and exposing conspiracies, but significant nonetheless.

The consultant returned with several belt options. As Mallory tried them against the dress, her phone vibrated in the robe pocket where she'd tucked it. She resisted the urge to check it immediately—Jen would kill her if she got distracted by work now—but her mind immediately wondered if it was Tucker, or perhaps Reynolds, with an update on the case.

"This one," Jen decided, pointing to a delicate crystal belt that caught the light beautifully. "It's perfect."

Mallory nodded her agreement, and the consultant began making notes about the necessary alterations. Jen snapped a few photos, 'for Mom,' before the consultant helped Mallory back to the dressing room to change.

Once alone, Mallory checked her phone. A text from Tucker: "Lewis called. Wants to meet. No pressure."

She frowned slightly. Tucker's former FBI supervisor had been a shadow hovering at the edges of the Duckwood case, a reminder of Tucker's past and the incident that had prompted his resignation from the Bureau. What could Lewis want now?

Then there was Director Hargrove's surprising job offer, which they'd barely discussed. The idea of joining the FBI—working together on a specialized task force—was both intriguing and unsettling. It would mean leaving behind the independence they'd built, the flexibility of choosing their own cases and methods and, most of all, her family.

But it would also mean greater resources, a wider reach, the ability to tackle larger criminal networks than they could as private investigators. And if they were both offered positions, they wouldn't have to sacrifice their partnership.

These thoughts followed Mallory as she changed back into her regular clothes and rejoined Jen in the boutique's sitting area to complete the paperwork for her dress order.

"You're a million miles away," Jen observed as they left the boutique. "What's going on in that head of yours?"

Mallory hesitated, then decided her sister deserved the truth. "Tucker got a job offer. From the FBI. For both of us, actually."

Jen's eyes widened. "The FBI? Like, moving to Washington?"

"Possibly. It's for a new task force focused on weapons trafficking. After the Duckwood case, we apparently got their attention."

"Wow." Jen processed this as they walked to their cars. "How do you feel about it?"

"Conflicted," Mallory admitted. "It's a tremendous opportunity, of course. But..."

"But you've built a life here," Jen finished the thought. "The agency with Tucker, the wedding plans, being close to your family."

Mallory nodded. "Exactly. And Tucker left the FBI for a good reason. Going back would mean sacrificing some of the independence we value," she said as she followed her sister out into the parking lot.

Jen leaned against her car, studying her sister thoughtfully. "You know, when you started working with Tucker, I worried it was just another of your phases, like that year you decided to become a professional rock climber, or the six months you spent trying to launch a food blog."

"Thanks for the vote of confidence," Mallory replied dryly.

"But this was different," Jen continued, ignoring the sarcasm. "You found something that challenged you, that used your natural curiosity and persistence for something meaningful. And you found a partner who loves you."

"That's what I'm afraid of losing," Mallory confessed. "The way we work together as equals. In the Bureau, there would be a chain of command, protocols, all the things Tucker left behind."

Jen considered this. "Maybe. But you'd still be you, and Tucker would still be Tucker. The circumstances might change, but the core of what makes your partnership work doesn't have to."

It was surprisingly insightful coming from Jen, who typically focused more on practical concerns like wedding arrangements and social calendars than existential questions about career paths.

"When did you get so wise about relationships?" Mallory asked with a small smile.

"Twenty-four years of marriage teaches you a few things," Jen replied. "Like the fact that the right partnership can withstand changes in circumstance. Jared and I have moved three times, changed careers, had children—the external stuff shifts, but what matters is how you face it together."

Mallory hugged her sister impulsively. "Thanks. For the dress help and the life advice."

"Anytime," Jen said, returning the embrace. "Just promise me one thing: if you do move to Washington, you'll stay in touch?"

"Deal," Mallory laughed. "Hey, of course I will."

After saying goodbye to Jen, Mallory drove directly to the office, her mind clearer than it had been that morning. She found Tucker at his desk, the completed Fisher report printed and ready in a professional folder.

"Dress mission accomplished?" he asked, looking up from his computer.

"Mission accomplished. Even found one I actually like." She set her purse down and perched on the edge of his desk. "Your text said Lewis called?"

Tucker nodded, his expression neutral. "Wants to meet for coffee. Says he has information relevant to Hargrove's offer."

"Are you going to go?"

"I thought we might go together," Tucker replied. "Since the offer concerns both of us."

Mallory studied him, noting the tension around his eyes. "Are you considering it? The FBI position?"

Tucker leaned back in his chair, his expression thoughtful. "I'm considering considering it. Which means at least I'll listen to what Lewis has to say."

"That's... surprisingly open-minded, coming from you," she said, her head tilted to one side.

"Yes, well. Detective Bradley said something yesterday that stuck with me," Tucker admitted. "About not letting the job consume everything else. About balance."

Mallory remembered the exchange at the nursing home, how the retired detective had looked meaningfully at her when giving Tucker advice about life priorities.

"You think rejoining the FBI would help with that balance?" she asked skeptically.

"Not necessarily. But making decisions based solely on old grudges might not be the best approach either." Tucker met her gaze directly. "What about you? You've been quiet about the offer."

Mallory considered her conversation with Jen. "I'm intrigued by the opportunity. But I don't want to lose what we've built here, as partners, as investigators who can choose our own path."

"I share that concern," Tucker acknowledged. "But I'm also thinking about impact. What we could accomplish with federal resources behind us."

"Like taking down larger criminal networks than we can reach as private investigators," she said.

"Exactly." Tucker stood, moving to the window that overlooked downtown Chattanooga. "The Duckwood case was bigger than we initially thought, a decade-and-a-half-long operation with connections to international weapons suppliers. And that was in a town of less than thirteen thousand people."

Mallory understood his point. Their work as private investigators was meaningful, but inherently limited in scope. "So we meet with Lewis, hear what he has to say. No commitments, just information gathering."

"Agreed. He suggested tomorrow morning at the coffee shop down the street."

"Works for me," Mallory said, then changed the subject. "Did you finish the Fisher report?"

Tucker nodded, handing her the folder. "Complete account of what we found, who was responsible for Terry's murder, and how it connected to the other victims. I've anonymized some of Tanya's contributions for her protection, but everything else is there."

Mallory scanned the report, impressed, as always, by Tucker's thorough documentation. Every detail was captured, from their initial meeting with Gary through the raid on the Parsons farm and the subsequent arrests.

"It's good work," she said.

"Thank you," Tucker said. "I also called Reynolds this morning. They've located the murder weapon used on Terry Fisher."

Mallory looked up sharply. "Where?"

"Pearcy's storage unit. Along with weapons used in the other murders. He kept them as some kind of twisted trophies."

"So Pearcy himself pulled the trigger? On all five victims?"

Tucker nodded grimly. "Ballistics confirmed it. He didn't just orchestrate the murders—he committed them personally."

Mallory processed this new information. "The mild-mannered pastor was actually the executioner," she said. "No wonder he had a psychological break when it all started coming apart."

"His confession at the storage unit makes more sense now. He talked about the victims as 'sinners' who needed to be eliminated for the greater good. In his mind, he was delivering judgment."

"Religious justification for cold-blooded murder," Mallory said, shaking her head. "People can rationalize anything."

They spent the next hour reviewing case notes and organizing their files, the routine work of closing an investigation. It felt almost anticlimactic after the intensity of the past week, but Mallory welcomed the return to normalcy.

Eventually, Tucker suggested they call it a day. "Dinner? I owe you a proper meal after all those burger dinners in Duckwood."

"I'd like that," Mallory agreed, gathering her things. "Somewhere with tablecloths and wine glasses."

"I know just the place," he replied.

They ended up at a small Italian restaurant overlooking the Tennessee River, with a view of the lights reflecting on the water as evening fell. Tucker had made a reservation, surprising Mallory with his foresight.

"Planning ahead?" she teased as they were seated at a window table.

"Occasionally," he replied with the hint of a smile. "Especially for important occasions."

"And what occasion is this?"

"The end of another case," he replied "Plus, you found a wedding dress today. That's worth celebrating, too."

Mallory laughed, feeling the tension of the past days finally easing. "When you put it that way, we definitely deserve wine."

Over dinner, they deliberately avoided discussing the FBI offer, focusing instead on lighter topics—the upcoming wedding, a film they'd been meaning to see, plans for a short honeymoon. It felt good to remember there was more to their relationship than work, more to life than investigations and danger.

As they finished dessert—a tiramisu they shared—Tucker reached across the table and took her hand in his. "Whatever we decide about Hargrove's offer, we decide together. As partners. That doesn't change."

"I know," Mallory said, squeezing his hand. "That's what matters most to me—that we face these choices as a team."

"Agreed." Tucker's expression softened in a way few people ever saw. "Detective Bradley was right about one thing—the cases will always be there. The people we care about should come first."

For Tucker, this was practically a declaration of love, and Mallory felt its significance. "Does this mean you'll actually have opinions about wedding details now?"

"Let's not get carried away," he replied dryly. "I'm still delegating most of that to you and Jen. But I'll make the decisions about cake."

"Fair enough." Mallory smiled, feeling a certainty settle over her. Whatever they decided about the FBI offer, whatever challenges came next, they would face them together. That was the partnership they'd built—one strong enough to weather changing circumstances while maintaining its essential balance.

Later that night, as they prepared for bed, Mallory found

herself thinking about the contrast between the darkness they'd encountered in Duckwood and the light they were building in their own lives.

"You're quiet," Tucker observed as he set his alarm for the morning.

"I was just thinking about how we spend our days investigating the worst of humanity, then come home to this."

Tucker considered this. "Maybe that's what makes our partnership work. We've seen enough darkness to appreciate the light. To protect it."

"Is that what you think the FBI task force would be? Protecting the light by fighting larger shadows?"

"Potentially," Tucker acknowledged. "But there are many ways to make that kind of difference. We'll know more after talking to Lewis tomorrow."

Mallory nodded, setting aside the question for now.

Tucker turned off the bedside lamp and reached for her.

In the darkness, Mallory felt Tucker's hand find hers.

TUCKER AND MALLORY arrived at the coffee shop ten minutes early the following morning, a habit Tucker had developed during his FBI days. The small café near their office was busy with the morning rush, but they secured a corner table that offered some privacy while still allowing Tucker to observe the entrance.

"Are you sure you're okay with this?" Mallory asked, noting the tension in Tucker's shoulders. "Meeting with Lewis again?"

"I'm not too bothered about it," Tucker said. "He's a total... He's... Well, avoiding him doesn't serve any purpose if we're seriously considering Hargrove's offer."

The door opened, and David Lewis entered the café. He

hadn't changed much since Tucker had last worked with him. His hair was a little grayer at the temples, the lines around his eyes had deepened, but he still carried himself with the confident bearing of a senior FBI official. He spotted them immediately and approached after ordering a coffee at the counter.

"Tucker. Ms. Carver." Lewis nodded to each of them as he took the third seat at their table. "Thank you for agreeing to meet with me."

Tucker acknowledged him with a neutral nod, then dove right in. "You said you had some information about Director Hargrove's offer and the task force."

Lewis took a sip of his coffee before responding. "I do. I've been tasked with helping structure the operation. Hargrove wants it to function differently from traditional Bureau units. He wants it to be more flexible, less bureaucratic. Similar to how you two operate, actually."

"Why the sudden interest in our methods?" Mallory asked directly. "The Bureau isn't exactly known for embracing independent approaches."

Lewis's expression shifted to something Tucker hadn't seen often during their time working together, a genuine reflection.

"The landscape is changing, Ms. Carver. Traditional approaches haven't been effective against the cartels and their sophisticated weapons trafficking networks. What you accomplished in Duckwood in just a matter of days was impressive and something that's eluded federal task forces for years in similar situations."

"Because we weren't constrained by bureaucracy," Tucker pointed out.

"Exactly," Lewis agreed, surprising Tucker with his candor. "Which is why Hargrove wants to create a unit that operates with similar autonomy within the Bureau framework."

Tucker studied his former supervisor carefully. "And you're

on board with this approach? You were never a fan of operational flexibility when we worked together."

Lewis set down his coffee cup, meeting Tucker's gaze directly. "People change, Tucker. Perspectives evolve. The Marsha Cline case... I know how it changed you..." He paused, then said, "It changed things for me too."

The mention of Cline's name hung in the air between them. Tucker remained silent, waiting.

"You were right," Lewis continued after a moment. "We moved too soon. I overruled your assessment because I was concerned about the optics, about how a delayed operation would look in the report. It was the wrong call, and it cost that young woman her life."

Mallory glanced at Tucker, sensing the significance of this admission. Tucker's expression remained neutral, but his posture had shifted slightly.

"Why tell me this now?" Tucker asked.

"Because if you're going to consider returning to the Bureau in any capacity, you deserve to know that lessons were learned from that incident." Lewis leaned forward slightly. "Your resignation prompted a review of tactical decision-making protocols. Changes were implemented. I was reassigned temporarily, required to undergo additional training before returning to a supervisory position."

Tucker hadn't known this. He'd left the Bureau immediately after the incident, cutting all ties. "I wasn't aware of that."

"You wouldn't have been," Lewis acknowledged. "The Bureau doesn't publicize its internal corrective measures. But your principled stand had an impact."

Mallory interjected, bringing the conversation back to the present. "What exactly would this new task force do? And what would our roles be?"

Lewis seemed grateful for the shift. "The task force would

focus on identifying and dismantling domestic weapons trafficking operations, particularly those with connections to international suppliers, like the cartels. Your roles would be as lead field investigators, with authority to determine operational approaches within broad parameters."

"Reporting structure?" Tucker asked.

"Direct line to Deputy Director Kaminski, bypassing regional supervision," Lewis explained. "You'd have access to Bureau resources, intelligence, and tactical support when needed, but day-to-day operations would be at your discretion."

"And you?" Tucker asked bluntly. "Where do you fit in this hierarchy?"

Lewis met his gaze evenly. "I'd be a resource, not a supervisor. My role would be liaison between the task force and other Bureau departments. I wouldn't have operational authority over your investigations."

Tucker nodded, filing this information away. "Location?" he asked.

"Flexible. The task force would have a nominal headquarters in Washington, but field operations could be run from regional offices. You could potentially remain based at the Chattanooga field office, traveling as cases required."

Mallory leaned forward. "And my role specifically? I'm not former Bureau. I don't have the training Tucker does."

"That's precisely why Hargrove wants you," Lewis replied. "Your background, including your three years as a private investigator and Tucker's partner, brings a different perspective, different methods. The Bureau needs that fresh approach. You'd receive abbreviated tactical training, but you had a good teacher in Tucker. Your investigative skills are already proven."

They continued discussing operational details for another thirty minutes: budget allocations, personnel support, jurisdictional considerations. Lewis was surprisingly forthcoming, providing specific information rather than the vague assurances Tucker had expected.

As the meeting wound down, Lewis reached into his brief-case and withdrew two folders. "The official offers, with complete details. No pressure to decide immediately. Hargrove said to give you two weeks."

Tucker accepted the folders without opening them. "We'll review them carefully," he said.

Lewis stood to leave, then hesitated. "For what it's worth, Tucker, I hope you'll consider it. The Bureau needs people who stand by their principles, even when it's uncomfortable. Especially then."

After Lewis departed, Tucker and Mallory remained at the table, the folders between them.

"That was unexpected," Mallory said finally. "He actually admitted he was wrong about the Cline case."

Tucker nodded, still processing the conversation. "People can surprise you, sometimes."

"Are you considering it more seriously now?"

Tucker met her gaze. "I'm considering it with an open mind. Lewis's admission changes the context somewhat. But what matters is what we want for our future, not what the Bureau needs."

Mallory placed her hand over his. "Whatever we decide, we decide together."

Tucker nodded, picking up the folders. They had a lot to discuss.

EPILOGUE

SIX MONTHS LATER

THE CHATTANOOGA BOTANICAL Gardens in late April was a glorious cacophony of cherry blossoms and dogwoods creating a canopy of white and pink, azaleas adding splashes of vibrant color along the winding paths. A white tent had been erected in the central garden, rows of chairs arranged in neat semicircles facing an arch woven with fresh spring flowers.

Tucker stood beneath the arch, adjusting his cuffs for the third time in as many minutes. Nate, his brother, leaned closer, speaking in a low voice only Tucker could hear.

"Relax. You've faced armed criminals with less anxiety than this."

"Different kind of stress," Tucker replied, scanning the assembled guests. Ninety-five people—mostly Mallory's extended family and friends, with a smaller contingent from Tucker's side. His parents in the front row, his former FBI colleagues scattered throughout, even David Lewis sitting near the back.

The decision about Hargrove's offer had not been easy. Their meeting with Lewis had revealed more nuance than Tucker expected—a restructuring at the Bureau, greater autonomy for specialized task forces, even an admission from Lewis that his call in the Marsha Cline case had been wrong. The conversation had opened a door to healing old wounds, though Tucker still carried the scars of that tragic outcome.

In the end, they'd surprised everyone, including themselves, by proposing an alternative: they would consult for the FBI task force from Chattanooga, maintaining their private agency while lending their expertise to specific weapons trafficking cases. Hargrove had eventually agreed, recognizing the value of their independence and local connections.

The arrangement had worked surprisingly well for the past five months. They still chose their own cases, but occasionally traveled to assist the task force with investigations that benefited from their specialized knowledge. It was the balance they'd sought; impact on a larger scale without sacrificing the partnership dynamic they'd built.

The string quartet began a new piece, signaling the ceremony was about to begin. Tucker straightened, his attention drawn to the garden path where the bridal party would appear. First came Jen, resplendent in a deep blue dress that complemented the spring setting, followed by Mallory's niece Jackie and two friends from college.

Then the music shifted, and the assembled guests rose. Tucker's breath caught as Mallory appeared on her father's arm.

She was radiant in a simple but elegant gown, her hair swept up with a few strategic curls framing her face. She carried a bouquet of spring flowers that matched the arch above Tucker's head. But it was her expression that held him transfixed; confident, joyful, her eyes finding his immediately across the distance.

As she approached, Tucker was struck by how this moment crystallized everything they'd built together.

Mallory reached the arch and her father placed her hand in Tucker's before stepping back. Up close, he could see the faint scar above her eyebrow from a case last year, the determined set of her jaw that had faced down criminals and bureaucrats alike, the intelligence and compassion in her eyes that made her such an effective investigator.

"You look beautiful," he whispered.

"You clean up pretty well yourself," she replied with a smile. "No ankle holster under those pants, I hope?"

"Nate made me leave it in the car," Tucker admitted, drawing a soft laugh from her.

"You sure you want to do this?" she whispered.

There was a moment of silence. She nudged him. "Hey, I was joking."

"I know you were," he muttered.

"Well?" she persisted.

"Of course I do."

The officiant began the ceremony, but Tucker found himself only partially attending to the words. His mind flashed through moments from their partnership: their first case together, the gradual shift from colleagues to something more, the Duckwood investigation that had tested and ultimately strengthened their bond.

When the time came for vows, they had opted for simple, traditional words rather than writing their own—neither of them comfortable with public displays of emotion. Yet the standard phrases carried deeper meaning given all they had faced together: for better or worse, in sickness and health, until death do us part.

They had already proven their commitment through gunfire, danger, and difficult choices. This ceremony merely formalized what had been true for some time. They were partners in every sense of the word, stronger together than apart.

The exchange of rings, the official pronouncement, the kiss that sealed their union, all passed in a blur of emotion Tucker hadn't fully anticipated. Then they were walking back down the aisle together, husband and wife, greeted by applause and smiling faces.

The reception unfolded beneath the white tent, now configured with round tables and a small dance floor. Tucker had indeed chosen the cake, a simple three-tier design with fresh flowers matching Mallory's bouquet. True to his nature, he had researched cake options methodically, even creating a spreadsheet comparing flavors, textures, and prices before making his selection.

As guests enjoyed dinner and drinks, Tucker found himself approached by Gary Fisher, who had traveled from Duckwood with his parents for the wedding.

"Mr. Randall, or should I say, Agent Randall now?" Gary extended his hand. "Congratulations."

"Thank you," Tucker replied, shaking his hand. "And it's still just Tucker. We're consultants, not agents."

"Consultant, investigator, whatever the title, I'm grateful for your work." Gary glanced toward his parents, seated at a nearby table. "Dad's holding steady. The doctors say he might have another year, maybe more. Having answers about Terry made a huge difference."

"I'm glad to hear that," Tucker said sincerely. "How is Duckwood recovering?"

Gary considered the question. "Slowly. Trust doesn't come back overnight. The new police chief is working hard to rebuild community relations. Pastor Williams at the Whitehaven Baptist church is too. He's young, energetic, and determined to heal the wounds Pearcy left."

"And Tanya?" Tucker asked, lowering his voice. "Any word?"

"Witness protection program," Gary replied quietly. "Reynolds says she's doing well in her new location. She testified against Parsons and Winson last month: airtight cases, both of them."

"Good. She deserves peace after everything she did to bring the truth to light."

The conversation shifted to lighter topics—Gary's children, Tucker's consulting work, the botanical garden setting. After Gary moved on to greet Mallory, Tucker found himself momentarily alone, watching the celebration unfold around him.

His gaze found Mallory at the far side of the tent, deep in conversation with his parents. She laughed at something his father said, her whole face lighting up. Tucker felt a profound gratitude in that moment, for the partnership they'd built, for the balance they maintained, for the simple fact that they had both survived the dangers their work entailed.

As if sensing his attention, Mallory looked up, meeting his eyes across the distance. A silent communication passed between them, the same wordless understanding that had served them so well in investigations now connecting them in this personal moment.

The band began playing a slow song, and Tucker crossed to where Mallory stood, extending his hand in invitation. She took it with a smile, allowing him to lead her to the dance floor for their first dance as husband and wife.

"Happy?" he asked as they moved together to the music.

"Very," she confirmed. "Though Jen is already asking when we're going to start thinking about children."

Tucker raised an eyebrow. "I assume you told her we're a bit busy now, consulting for the FBI and running a private investigation agency."

"Something like that," Mallory laughed. "I told her we're taking one major life change at a time."

They danced in comfortable silence for a moment before Tucker spoke again. "I received a letter from Marsha Cline's parents yesterday."

Mallory looked up in surprise. After the Duckwood case, Tucker had finally told her the full story of the hostage situation that had gone wrong, the nineteen-year-old victim who had died because of a premature breach, the guilt he had carried for years afterward. And, with her encouragement, he'd reached out to the victim's family.

"What did they say?" she asked gently.

"That they appreciated hearing from me after all this time. That they've found some measure of peace. That they're glad I've found the same." Tucker's voice was steady, but Mallory could feel the emotion beneath his words. "They're good people. They didn't have to respond so graciously."

"Some wounds heal with time and truth," Mallory said, resting her head against his shoulder. "Like the Fisher family. Like Duckwood, eventually."

"Like my own," Tucker acknowledged quietly.

The song ended, and other couples joined them on the dance floor. Mallory's father claimed her for the traditional father-daughter dance, while Tucker found himself partnered with his mother.

The celebration continued as evening fell, lights twinkling in the tent and throughout the gardens. Tucker and Mallory circulated among their guests, accepting congratulations and sharing moments with those who had traveled to witness their union.

As the reception began winding down, Tucker spotted Reynolds in conversation with Lewis near the cake table. The two men had developed an effective working relationship during the prosecution of the Duckwood conspirators, despite initial jurisdictional tensions.

"Admiring your cake selection?" Mallory asked, joining Tucker as he watched them.

"Monitoring potential interdepartmental conflict," he replied with a hint of humor. "Old habits."

"Always the investigator," she teased, taking his hand. "Even at our wedding."

"Occupational hazard." Tucker said and squeezed her hand gently. "Ready to make our exit soon? The hotel's sending a car."

Mallory nodded. "Almost. There's just one more thing I need to do."

She slipped away, returning to the bridal suite briefly before reappearing with a small, wrapped package. She handed it to Tucker with a smile that held just a hint of mischief.

"What's this?" he asked, weighing the package in his hand.

"Open it and see."

Tucker unwrapped the gift carefully, revealing a leather-bound notebook similar to the ones he used for case notes, but of finer quality. Opening the cover, he found an inscription on the first page in Mallory's distinctive handwriting:

For our next chapter. The best partnerships evolve, but never lose their balance. All my love, Mallory.

Below the inscription was a photograph he'd never seen before. It was of the two of them at a crime scene early in their partnership, heads bent together over evidence, completely focused on the work but also unmistakably in sync. Tucker couldn't recall who had taken the picture, but it captured perfectly the foundation of their relationship.

"How did you get this?" he asked, genuinely surprised. Tucker was not easy to surprise.

"Nate had it. Apparently, one of the officers at that scene was his friend from the academy. He thought we made an interesting pair and snapped the photo. Nate held onto it, thinking it might be significant someday. And then he gave it to me."

"He has good instincts," Tucker said, carefully re-wrapping the gift and tucking it into his jacket pocket. "Thank you." And he leaned forward and kissed her.

The final hour of the reception passed quickly—the bouquet toss—caught by Jackie, to Jen's visible alarm—the cake cutting —executed with Tucker's typical precision—and finally, the sparkler send-off as they departed for their hotel.

In the quiet of the car, Mallory leaned against Tucker's shoulder, her expression peaceful. "We did it," she said simply.

"The wedding? Or the past six months of juggling FBI consultations, private cases, and wedding planning?"

"All of it," Mallory replied. "Every bit. We did it."

"We did," he agreed, his arm tightening around her shoulders. "And we'll keep doing it, whatever comes next."

Detective Bradley's words came back to Tucker as the car carried them away from the celebration: "The cases will always be there, but the people we care about won't." He had taken that wisdom to heart, finding a way to pursue justice while prioritizing what mattered most.

The balance they'd achieved wasn't perfect, and it would require constant attention to maintain. But as Tucker looked at Mallory beside him, he knew without a doubt that they would succeed.

"By the way," he said, turning to look at her, "what are we going to call the business now we're married? Randall & Mrs. Randall?"

She made a face, then said, "Randall & Carver will do just fine."

AUTHOR'S NOTE:

While this story is loosely based on actual happenings, it is a work of fiction. Duckwood, TN, doesn't exist. I set it in Cumberland County because it's a beautiful area and I know it quite well having played a lot of golf up there when I was a journalist.

As to Chattanooga: there are, of course, no botanical gardens, though I think there should be. So why set the wedding there? Well, because I thought it would be nice.

TURN THE PAGE
TO FIND
MORE
GREAT BOOK SERIES
FROM
BLAIR HOWARD!

From Blair Howard

The Harry Starke Genesis Series
9 Books in Series as of 2025

The Harry Starke Series
24 Books in Series as of 2025

The Lt. Kate Gazzara Murder Files
21 Books in Series as of 2025

Randall And Carver Mysteries
3 Books in Series as of 2025

The Peacemaker Series
3 Books in Series as of 2025

The O'Sullivan Chronicles: Civil War Series
5 Books in Series as of 2025

From Blair C. Howard

The Sovereign Star Series
7 Books in Series as of 2025

Also available in German

ABOUT THE AUTHOR

Blair Howard is a retired journalist turned novelist. He's the author of more than 50 novels including the international best-selling Harry Starke series of detective crime stories, the Lt. Kate Gazzara Police Procedural series, the Harry Starke Genesis series, and the Randall & Carver Mysteries. He's also the author of the Peacemaker series of international spy thrillers and five Civil War/Western novels.

If you enjoy reading Science Fiction thrillers, Mr. Howard has made his debut into the genre with, The Sovereign Stars Series under the name, Blair C. Howard.

www.BlairHowardBooks.com

www.ingramcontent.com/pod-product-compliance
Lightning Source LLC
Chambersburg PA
CBHW011406010726
47495CB00009B/2793